Witch Is Why The Search Began

Published by Implode Publishing Ltd
© Implode Publishing Ltd 2017

Chapter 1

"Morning, Jill," Mrs V and Jules chorused.

"Morning. Isn't it your day off, Jules?"

"Yeah. I'm meeting Gilbert in town in a few minutes, but I wanted to be here so that Annabel and I could tell you our news."

"Oh? And what's that?"

"We've reached an agreement on the colour for the office," Mrs V said.

"That's great. Really great."

I had hoped that the stalemate over what colour to redecorate the office might last a while longer. I was in no hurry to fork out money that I didn't have, just to spruce the place up. Still, I'd made them a promise, and there was no going back on it now.

"We've decided on sky blue," Mrs V said. "It will brighten this place up a treat. What colour will you have your office painted, Jill?"

"I hadn't really thought about it. Black probably. Or purple."

They both had the same horrified expression.

"Only joking. I guess I'll stick with something boring. Magnolia most likely."

"How quickly will you be able to get someone in?" Mrs V was obviously keen.

"I'm not sure. I'll try to get on it later today. How was your weekend?"

"Armi and I went to the Ever ballroom yesterday," Mrs V said. "We had a wonderful time. You haven't seen Armi's paso doble, have you, Jill?"

"Not lately."

"It's something to behold."

"What about you, Jules? You were going to ToppersCon, weren't you?"

Her smile dissolved. "I'm trying to forget about that."

"Bad?"

"Worse. Much worse. I was the only 'normal' person there. I mean, what kind of people spend their time collecting bottle tops? And when they get talking to one another, it's the best cure for insomnia known to man."

"That bad, eh?"

"Oh, yes. And trust us to get stuck with the most boring man there. This funny little guy who writes the Toppers Newsletter latched onto us, and we couldn't get rid of him."

"You mean Mr Ivers."

"Yeah, that's him. How did you know?"

"He used to be one of my neighbours. He was into movies back then. He works at the toll bridge in Smallwash."

"He's insufferable. He even tried to get us to subscribe to his stupid newsletter, but I said we couldn't afford it. I mean, who in their right mind would pay to receive a newsletter from that nut job?"

Who indeed?

"And just look at this." Jules reached into her bag, and brought out a silk scarf with a 'bottle top' print. "Gilbert bought this for me while I was getting a coffee."

"It's — err — quite a nice colour. I suppose."

"It's hideous. I wouldn't be seen dead in it. Would you like it, Jill? It's more your kind of thing."

"No, thanks. I'm not very big on scarves. Do you and Gilbert have anything exciting planned for today?"

"He doesn't know it yet, but we're going to call in at Yarnstormers."

"I didn't realise they were open for business."

"They're opening today, and they're giving away a free pair of knitting needles to every customer. I'm going to get Gilbert to grab some too—that way I end up with two pairs."

"I bet he'll be thrilled at being dragged into a wool shop on his day off."

"I don't care. After what I had to put up with this weekend, it's the least he can do."

"What about you, Mrs V? Are you planning on checking out Ever's new competitor?"

"Of course, dear. I shall have a walk over there during my lunch break. You're welcome to come with me, if you like?"

"No, thanks. I'll give it a miss. If Grandma sees me go in there, she'll have my guts for garters."

***

Winky was standing next to the window.

"Do, Re, Mi, Fa, Sol, La, Ti, Do. Do, Re, Mi, Fa, Sol, La, Ti, Do."

"What are you doing, Winky?"

"What does it sound like?"

"The cat's chorus."

"That's because you don't have an ear for a fine voice. Do, Re, Mi, Fa, Sol, La, Ti, Do."

"What's all this in aid of?"

"I'm practising for the competition later this week."

"What competition?"

"The Feline Choir Competition."

"It really is the cat's chorus, then." I laughed.

"I don't know what you find so amusing. I'll have you know that we've won best feline choir for the last two years."

"You've never mentioned any of this before."

"You know me. I like to keep my light well and truly hidden under a bushel."

"Where is the competition being held?"

"Washbridge Arena."

"They hire the place out to cats?"

"Of course they don't, and besides, who'd pay to rent that fleapit? It's closed for refurbishment, so we're going to take advantage before the workmen move in. When we win this time, we get to keep the trophy for good."

"*When you win*? Isn't that rather presumptuous?"

"Not at all. The other choirs can't hold a candle to us." He took a deep breath. "Do, Re, Mi, Fa, Sol, La, Ti, Do."

"I'm sorry, but I can't listen to that row all day long. I have a lot on my mind, like trying to figure out where to find the money to get these offices redecorated."

"Not before time. This room could do with a lick of paint." He glanced around. "Tangerine might be nice."

"I'm not working in an office painted tangerine."

"Magenta then?"

"Definitely not. I thought magnolia."

"I might have known."

"What do you mean by that?"

"That you'd choose a colour as boring as you are."

"I am not boring."

He yawned.

"I'm not, and besides, I might not be able to afford to

get it done at all."

"It needn't cost you a fortune. You should stick it on Find-A-Painter."

"On what?"

"You must have seen it. It's a website where you get a number of tradesmen to give you a quote for the work you need doing. There's a whole series of them: Find-A-Plumber, Find-An-Electrician, Find-A-Cheese Sculptor."

"Who would ever need a cheese sculptor?"

"How would I know?" He shrugged. "But if you ever do, I'm guessing that Find-A- Cheese Sculptor would be the place to start."

I brought up the Find-A-Painter website on my computer. It was all very straightforward. It only took me a few minutes to snap a couple of photos of both offices, upload them, and enter details of the work I needed doing.

"There. All done. Thanks for the tip, Winky."

"No problem. Do, Re, Mi, Fa, Sol, La, Ti, Do. Do, Re, Mi, Fa, Sol, La, Ti, Do."

***

Half an hour later, Mrs V came through to my office. Thankfully, by then, Winky had decided to give the voice exercises a rest.

"Jill, I have a Mr Anthony Coultard to see you. He doesn't have an appointment, but he says that you know him."

"Coultard?" The name didn't ring a bell.

"He said to mention that he owns the antique jeweller's shop."

"Of course. Send him through." I'd consulted Anthony Coultard when trying to find out more information about my locket.

"Thank you for seeing me without an appointment, Jill. I remembered your name, and found your address in the phone book."

"No problem. Please have a seat."

"Thank you. I must say that receptionist of yours is something rather special?"

"Mrs V?"

"Is she married?"

"No, but she is seeing someone."

"Pity. Is it serious?"

"I think so."

"Just my luck." Just then Winky jumped onto the sofa. "Is that your cat?"

"Yeah. That's Winky."

"Winky, eh? I used to have a cat with no ears."

"What did you call it?"

"Anything I liked. It couldn't hear a word I said." He erupted into laughter. "Just my little joke. Your boy really is a handsome beast. I bet all the lady cats are after him."

"What exactly was it you needed my help with, Mr Coultard?"

"You must call me Ant. The thing is, Jill, I didn't really know who to go to with this. I had an approach last Friday from what I could only describe as a shady character."

"Shady how?"

"You know the sort. Pick your pocket while talking to you, given half a chance. Anyway, this spiv comes into my shop and asks if I'm interested in buying fairy wings. Starlight fairy wings, to be precise. I assume you're familiar with the starlight fairies?"

"I am. When I first heard that people collected their wings, I was horrified until I realised that they were wings that had been shed by the fairies."

"That's just the problem, Jill. The legitimate dealers only trade in 'shed' wings, but regrettably there is also a black market for 'unshed' wings."

"Unshed?" I felt an involuntary shiver run through my body. "Surely you can't mean—?"

"I'm afraid I do. Fairies are being killed for their wings."

"That's terrible. Is that what this 'spiv' was selling?"

"He didn't come right out and say so, but reading between the lines, I'm pretty sure that's the case."

"What did you do?"

"I told him I wasn't interested, but he was very pushy. According to him, several of his clients are making a small fortune from selling them. I told him to get lost or I'd knock his block off. After he'd left, I couldn't get it out of my mind. Those poor, innocent fairies. Obviously, I couldn't take this to the police, but then I thought of you."

"I'm as horrified about this as you are, but I'm not sure what I can do. How would I even find this guy?"

"When he was trying to convince me to change my mind, he mentioned a particular shop in Washbridge that is doing a roaring trade in the wings. It's called Shiny Shiny. I thought maybe you could pay them a visit, and see if you could track him down from there."

"Okay. I'll check them out. If I can help to shut down this awful trade then of course I will."

***

Long after Ant Coultard had left, I was still thinking about the poor starlight fairies. What kind of person would kill a fairy just to get their wings?

My phone rang, but I didn't recognise the number.

"Jill? It's Megan."

"Hi there."

"Look, I thought you'd want to know that there's something strange going on in your house."

"What do you mean, strange?"

"I can hear music, loud voices and laughter coming from in there. Neither of your cars were on the drive, so I knew it couldn't be you or Jack. I just thought I ought to let you know."

"Right. Thanks."

"Do you want me to go around there to check what's going on?"

"No. Better not. I'm on my way."

It would have taken too long to drive home. If it was burglars, they'd be long gone before I got back. I didn't want to magic myself directly into the house without first finding out what I was getting into, so instead, I aimed for the back garden.

"Jill?"

Oh bum! Megan was in her garden.

"Hi. Thanks for calling me."

"How did you get back so quickly? I've only just finished on the call."

"As luck would have it, I was already on my way home. I was only a couple of streets away when you called."

"I didn't hear your car."

"My car? I—err—I thought it best to park in the next street, so as not to alert whoever is inside."

"Good thinking. Don't you think you should call the police?"

"No need. I'll be fine. Thanks again." I quickly made my way around the side of the house before she could ask any more awkward questions.

I could hear music and voices coming from inside, so I quietly opened the front door, and followed the sounds into the lounge.

"What's going on in here, Mrs Crustie?"

Agatha Crustie, my so-called cleaner, was sitting in the armchair. She had a glass of wine in one hand and a cake in the other. There were three other women in the room, all armed with drinks and cakes.

"Hello, Jill!" Agatha stood up. "Why don't you grab a glass? It's Cynthia's birthday, so we're having a bit of a knees-up."

"In my house? Drinking my wine and eating my cakes?"

"We didn't think you'd mind."

"Think again. I warned you about this."

"But it's Cynthia's birthday."

"I don't care. You're fired."

"You can't fire me."

"I just did. Take your friends, and get out of my house."

"You'll never get another cleaner once I let it be known how you've treated me."

"I'll take my chances. Now get out. All of you! And you can leave what's left of that bottle of wine behind."

Still chuntering about the injustice of it all, Agatha led her friends out of the house.

Good riddance!

Chapter 2

Back in Washbridge, I decided to grab a coffee, but I daren't go into Coffee Triangle in case they tried to foist that giant triangle on me again. Just the thought of it brought me out in a cold sweat. Instead, I grabbed a latte to-go from a small coffee shop, called Coff Drops. While I was in there, I bumped into Tonya from WashBets.

"Hi, Tonya, I believe you're dating Norman now?"

"Sorry. Do I know you?" She stared blankly at me.

"Not really. I've been in your shop a few times to see Ryan."

"If it was about a complaint, you should really have seen Bryan."

"Never mind."

The coffee was horrible. Sooner or later, I would have to find the courage to go back to Coffee Triangle. Giant triangle or no giant triangle.

"Jill!" Betty Longbottom called to me as I walked up the high street.

I'd hoped that I might avoid her for a while because she'd no doubt have it in for me after the Crustacean Monthly incident.

"Sorry, Betty. I can't stop. I have to get back to the office."

"I just wanted a quick word about what happened the other day when Crustacean Monthly were here."

Oh bum!

"I'm sorry about that, Betty. I didn't mean to—"

"No apology necessary. In fact, I want to thank you."

"You do?"

"Yes. I hadn't wanted Sid to feature in my profile, but it

seems I was wrong to be worried."

"You were?"

"Yes. It turns out that a lot of their readers like the 'bad-boy' look. Ever since the photos of Sid and I appeared, those readers have been travelling up here in droves, just to get a look at Sid. And, of course, while they're here, they spend lots of money in She Sells."

"That's great. I'm surprised the magazine is on the shelves so soon."

"It isn't. So far, the photos and a brief profile have only appeared online. Can you imagine how many more people are going to turn up when it's published?"

"What does Sid make of it all?"

"He doesn't say much, but he seems to like the attention." She gestured through the window; inside, Sid was leaning nonchalantly against a wall, surrounded by his admirers.

I carried on up the high street, and came upon a queue outside Yarnstormers. The opening offer of free knitting needles certainly seemed to be working. I was quite surprised that Grandma hadn't made an appearance. I'd expected her to have something to say about her new rival, but so far, nothing.

"If it isn't Jill Gooder." Ma Chivers appeared in front of me. "Has your grandmother sent you to spy on us?"

"I haven't seen or spoken to Grandma for a few days. I doubt she's afraid of a little competition."

"She should be. We've been as busy as this since we opened."

"Is Alicia working for you?"

"Don't mention that woman to me. After all the time I

spent tutoring her, she just ups and walks away without so much as a thank you."

"What is she doing now?"

"I don't know, and I don't care. The stupid girl says she's fallen in love. I gave her credit for more sense than that. Still, good riddance to bad rubbish, that's what I say."

Cyril poked his head out of the door. "I've finished pricing everything, Ma. What do you want me to do now?"

"You're late. You know I like my coffee every hour, on the hour. You're ten minutes late."

"Sorry, Ma. What would you like?"

"Why do you insist on asking me that every time. I'll have a flat white as usual, and make sure you go to Coffee Triangle. That muck you brought back from Coff Drops was revolting."

"Anything to eat with that?"

"Get me a chocolate brownie."

Cyril scurried off down the road.

"I see Cyril hasn't deserted you yet."

"Give him time. He'll no doubt turn out to be a disappointment, just like the others. Are you sure you don't want to come inside? I can give you the guided tour."

"No, thanks."

"I offered your sister the manager's job here, but she turned me down."

"That's because I told her to."

"I figured as much. She'll have you to blame when she finds herself out of a job, once we've seen Ever off."

"I wouldn't write off Grandma so soon if I were you."

As I walked back to the office, I pondered on what Ma Chivers had said about Alicia. Maybe she really had seen the light, and wanted to make a fresh start?

I still wasn't convinced.

***

"Look!" Mrs V held up a pair of knitting needles.

"From Yarnstormers?"

"Yes. They have a fabulous range of stock. I think they're going to give your grandmother a run for her money. They even have their own version of Everlasting Wool and One-Size Needles, and they're both cheaper."

That didn't bode well. Not one bit. Miles Best had tried to compete with Grandma, but that had been short-lived because his magic couldn't match hers. Ma Chivers was a different proposition. I doubted Grandma would be able to see her off so easily.

"What time is my next appointment, Mrs V?"

"Two-thirty. A Mr and Mrs Piper."

"Okay. That should give me time to sort out a few things first."

"Paperclips or rubber bands?"

Cheek! Why did I pay Mrs V to be so insubordinate? Oh wait, I didn't.

"Do, Re, Mi, Fa, Sol, La, Ti—" Winky crooned.

"No! Enough already! I can't take any more of that," I yelled.

"How am I supposed to prepare for the competition?" Winky looked a little put out, but I didn't care.

"You can do it tonight after I've gone home."

"Have you forgotten that I have the Midnight Gym to run overnight?"

"Do I look like I care?"

"You've changed. You're so hard these days."

"If that's true, you only have yourself to blame. You were the one who said I was a soft touch."

"Have you had any replies to your enquiry on Find-A-Painter?"

"I'll check." I logged onto the website. There were already two quotations, but neither of them was within my budget—not even close to it.

"You'll probably get more quotes overnight." Winky jumped onto the window sill.

"Unless they're a lot lower than this, it won't be happening."

At two-thirty on the dot, Mrs V showed in the Pipers—a couple in their forties. Mrs Piper looked like she'd spent at least two hours getting ready. Her husband had spent two minutes—tops.

"Mr and Mrs Piper. Nice to meet you both. Do have a seat. What can I do for you?"

"Thank you." Mr Piper held the seat for his wife. "Please call me Peter."

"And I'm Petra."

"Peter and Petra? You haven't lost a peck of pickled peppers by any chance?" I laughed.

They didn't. Instead, they looked rather surprised.

"How ever did you know?" Peter Piper said.

"We'd heard you were good, but frankly, that's incredible." Petra shook her head.

Huh?

"I'm sorry. I don't really follow. Perhaps you should start by telling me why you're here."

"It's just as you suggested," Peter said. "Someone has stolen the peppers."

"And the courgettes," his wife chipped in.

"Can we just rewind?" I was now mightily confused. "Where did the thefts take place?"

"We run a small, but rather exclusive restaurant in the *better* part of Washbridge," Petra said. "It's called Chez Piper. You've probably heard of it?"

"I don't think so."

They both looked disappointed in me.

"But then, I rarely eat out these days. I prefer to stay at home and cook."

"That's so refreshing. So few people cook these days. What's your speciality?"

Out of the corner of my eye, I could see Winky; he was grinning from ear to ear.

"Oh, you know. I like to mix it up. But enough about me. You were telling me about the thefts."

"Indeed." Peter picked up the story. "We spend a small fortune buying only the very best ingredients, and until recently, we've never had to worry about pilferage. All of our staff have been with us for several years, and we trust them all implicitly."

"I sense a 'but' coming?"

"But recently, there have been a number of thefts."

"Is it just food that is going missing, or has anything more valuable been taken?"

"It's only the food, and the total value isn't that great, but it's the worry that someone within our little operation is stealing. It's unnerved us."

"Have you reported the thefts to the police?"

"How could we? They aren't going to be interested in the theft of a few items of food. And anyway, we wouldn't want them to waste their resources on something like this, but we do want to get to the bottom of it."

"What did you want from me, exactly?"

"We thought that maybe you could spend some time working undercover at the restaurant. Hopefully, that will allow you to find out who is doing this."

"Are you sure? My fees will be much higher than the value of the food being stolen."

"Positive. You can't put a price on peace of mind."

"Okay. I'll be happy to help."

***

This was turning out to be quite a day. I'd already snagged two new clients, although I was unlikely to see any payment from the starlight fairy wings case. Not that that mattered—I simply couldn't have lived with myself if I didn't try to stop that awful trade.

Winky was itching to do more voice exercises, so I decided to pay Aunt Lucy a visit. She was always good for a cup of tea and a cake or three.

"I'm really sorry, Jill." Aunt Lucy was rushing around like a headless chicken. "I'm going shopping with some friends. They'll be here any minute."

"No problem. I just popped over on the off chance."

"You're welcome to make a cup of tea, and help yourself to cakes."

"I'll do that. I can catch up with Barry while I'm here. Is he okay? No more problems with the cat, I hope."

"I haven't seen anything of the cat since you scared it off. In fact, Barry is out in the garden now. I was intending to bring him in before I left, but if you're going to be here for a while, he can stay out there until you leave."

Just then, there was a knock at the door. Aunt Lucy let the two women in.

"Where's Gloria?" Aunt Lucy asked.

"She isn't coming," the taller of the two women said. "That stupid animal of hers has gone missing."

"Ladies, this is my niece, Jill. You've no doubt heard of her."

After we'd exchanged a few pleasantries, the three of them went on their way. I made myself a cup of tea, and grabbed a cherry cupcake. Through the kitchen window, I could see Barry, standing next to the gate at the far side of the garden. I was just about to go outside when I saw a young couple approach him. Barry stood with his front paws on the gate while the young woman took a selfie of the three of them.

How sweet.

They'd no sooner gone than another couple—middle-aged this time—approached Barry and took a selfie with him.

There was no way that could be a coincidence; something was afoot. Instead of going out of the back door, I went out the front way, and walked around to the gate. Once there, I had my answer.

Fastened to the gate was a notice which read:

Take selfie with cute dog, Barry. Price: five Barkies.

"Jill!" Barry jumped up, and put his front paws on the

gate. "Can we go for a walk?"

"Not just now." I took down the notice. "What's this all about?"

"I get Barkies for selfies."

"So I see. You didn't write this sign, did you? Who came up with this scheme?"

"Hamlet. It's good, isn't it?"

"No, it isn't. You're only meant to have a few Barkies each day. You'll be sick if you eat too many of them."

"But they're so tasty."

"They might be, but just because something is tasty doesn't mean you can spend all day eating it."

What? Don't be ridiculous. Custard creams and blueberry muffins are entirely different.

"Does that mean I can't have any more Barkies?" Barry sulked.

"Not today or you'll be poorly. I'm going to have a word with Hamlet. He has some explaining to do."

Chapter 3

I was surprised to find Hamlet running on his little wheel. He was usually reading a book or playing chess.

"Hamlet!"

No response.

"Hamlet!"

Still no response, but now I could see why; he had earphones in. I moved around to the front of the cage so I was in his line of sight, and tried again.

"Hamlet!"

This time he noticed me, took out the earphones, and stepped off the wheel.

"I'm sorry to disturb your exercise."

"Not a problem. I'd almost finished anyway."

"What music are you listening to?"

"Music? No. It's an audio book. Moby Dick. Have you read it?"

"Err—No, but I've seen the movie."

He rolled his eyes. "Not quite the same thing."

"I wanted a word about Barry."

"Which word did you have in mind? Boring? Tedious? Simple?"

"He told me that you suggested he should offer to be in selfies in exchange for Barkies."

"Yes? So?"

"It isn't good for him to eat too many Barkies. They'll make him ill."

"Then tell him to ask for money instead. My only concern is to get him out of my hair. How am I meant to concentrate on my reading when that big, soft lump keeps pestering me to read some childish book to him?"

"He just wants to be your friend."

"If you think you can make me feel guilty, you're mistaken. I already spend much more time with that stupid dog than you do, and you're supposed to be his owner."

Ouch! That stung, but he was right. I didn't spend nearly enough time with Barry.

"Okay, I'm sorry. I'm grateful that you spend so much time with him, but please don't encourage him to eat junk food."

"Message received and understood. Now, while you're here, I'd like you to do me a little favour."

"What's that?"

"My thirty-day free trial of RodentAudio is about to expire. I'd like you to set up a subscription for me."

"Pay for your audio books?"

"No. I don't expect you to pay; I just need you to set up the subscription using my credit card."

"How would I do that?"

"RodentAudio is run by Everything Rodent."

I should have known. Bill Ratman, the owner of Everything Rodent, seemed to have cornered the market in — err — well — everything rodent.

"Okay. Give me your card, and I'll go over there now."

***

I was the only customer in Everything Rodent. Bill Ratman was behind the counter, reading a book titled Of Rats and Men.

"Hello, young lady. I haven't seen you for a while."

"That's true, but I did recently pay a visit to Everything

Aquatic."

"I can't say I've heard of it."

"You'll never guess the name of the man who owns it?"

"Laurence?"

Huh? "No."

"Stewart? Brian?"

"No. His name is Bill Fishman." I waited for a reaction, but came there none, so I pressed on, "Don't you see? Bill Ratman — Bill Fishman?"

"Right." He smiled. "I get it. We're both called Bill. That is one heck of a coincidence."

There just weren't words.

"So, young lady, what can I help you with today?"

"Hamlet has been on the thirty-day free trial of RodentAudio, and would like to sign up for a subscription."

"Excellent. RodentAudio is really starting to take off. Which plan would he like?"

"There's more than one? He didn't say."

"The bronze plan will give him one book a month. The silver gives him three, and the gold gives him seven."

"He does get through a lot of books. How much do the different plans cost?"

"Eight pounds, fifteen pounds and twenty-five pounds respectively."

"Can he upgrade or downgrade later?"

"Sure."

"Okay. Sign him up for the silver plan for now."

"Will do. I just need his credit card."

While Bill went through the formalities of setting up the plan, I took a moment to reflect on my life. If three years ago, someone had told me that I'd be arranging an audio book subscription for my *hamster*, I would have thought they were certifiably insane. And yet, now it was just another day at the office. Perhaps I was the one who was insane. Or maybe one day I'd wake up in the shower, and discover the whole 'witch' thing had just been a dream.

"The card has been rejected." Bill Ratman's words brought me back down to earth.

"How do you mean?"

"The payment didn't go through. Do you have another card?"

"Only my own."

"We do take credit cards from the human world."

"How will the payment show on the statement?" I wasn't sure how I'd explain to Jack an entry which read 'Everything Rodent'.

"Don't worry. It will read BR Enterprises."

"Will I be able to change the card details when I've got this sorted out with Hamlet?"

"Of course. No problem."

"I suppose I'll have to do that, then. Change it to the Bronze plan though, would you?" I handed over my card.

When I got back to Aunt Lucy's house, there was no sign of the hamster.

"Where's Hamlet, Barry?"

"He said he was going to a book fair. I asked if I could go with him, but he said no."

"Did he say how long he'd be?"

Barry shook his head.

"I'm going to put Hamlet's credit card in his cage."

"Is it food? Can I have one?"

"No, it isn't food. Will you tell him that the card was

rejected?"

"Red what?"

"Rejected."

"Got it."

"Are you sure? What are you going to tell him?"

"That his card was red."

"Rejected."

"Red and ted."

"Never mind. Tell him I'll talk to him about it the next time I come over."

***

After that short but painful episode, I needed a muffin infusion.

"One of your best blueberry muffins, please, Amber."

"Sorry, Jill. We don't have any muffins, of any flavour."

"Very funny. Ha, ha."

"I'm not joking. Christy's Bakery had a problem with their electrics. They're going to be out of commission for a couple of days."

"Can't you get some from another supplier?"

"We did manage to get a few, but everyone is scrambling around trying to fill the gap that Christy's has left. The few we had were sold by mid-morning. It's a tragedy."

"I know. How am I meant to cope without a muffin?"

"I meant for Beryl."

"Who's Beryl?"

"Beryl Christy, of course."

"Oh yeah. Poor old Beryl."

"We do have a few brownies left." Amber pointed to the

pathetic selection in the display cabinet.

"Give me a chocolate one."

"Regular or double?"

"Do you have triple chocolate?"

"No."

"Double will have to do then. And a caramel latte."

"Have you asked Jill yet?" Pearl came charging over.

"I haven't had the chance," Amber said. "It's taken her ten minutes to choose a brownie."

"Tell me what?" I ignored Amber's uncalled-for jibe.

"About the seaside." Pearl gushed. "We're going on a day-trip tomorrow—Amber, Mum and me. Do you want to come with us?"

"I saw Aunt Lucy earlier—she never mentioned it, but then she was in a bit of a rush."

"We're going to Candle Sands. It's brilliant there. We always used to go when we were kids. You should definitely come."

"I do like the seaside, and it's been ages since I went. Aren't Alan and William going?"

"No. It's a girls' day out. Say you'll come, Jill. It'll be a laugh."

"Go on then. Why not?"

Daze and Blaze were seated near the window.

"Jill! Come and join us," Blaze called to me.

"Hi, you two."

"Hi." Daze barely managed a smile.

"What's wrong, Daze?"

"Nothing. I'm okay."

"You don't look it."

"She's annoyed about the new uniforms," Blaze said.

Daze shot him a withering look. "I told you I didn't want to talk about it."

"What's wrong with your catsuits?" I said. "I always thought they looked good."

"They do." She sighed. "But the powers-that-be have got it into their heads that we need a change. A *new image*." She used air quotes to emphasise her disdain.

"I quite like the new uniforms," Blaze said, sheepishly.

"You would!" she barked at him.

"What are they like?" I asked.

"Look." Blaze took a small, glossy leaflet out of his pocket, and placed it on the table.

"Oh dear. I'm not surprised you don't like this."

The leaflet showed two models wearing the proposed new rogue retriever costumes. The man was wearing what looked like a tracksuit; the woman was wearing a tight top and a mini-skirt. A micro-mini skirt.

"I'm not wearing that." Daze stabbed the leaflet with her finger.

"You have the legs for it," Blaze said.

"Shut up!" She slapped him down. "It doesn't matter whether or not I have the legs for it; it's demeaning. And besides, how am I meant to do my job in that? I'm not wearing it and that's that."

"But it's compulsory," Blaze said, in little more than a whisper.

"I don't care. I'm not wearing it, and if they don't like it, they'll just have to sack me."

Daze was livid, and I didn't blame her.

"I bet this was some man's idea," I said.

"Of course it was. I'd like to see him dressed like that. Anyway, enough of my woes. I'm sure you have problems of your own, Jill."

"No kidding. There isn't a muffin to be had in the place."

***

I was feeling quite chipper when I arrived home. The thought of a trip to the seaside had certainly lifted my spirits.

"You look very pleased with yourself," Jack said. He was in the kitchen, preparing dinner.

"I've had a good day at work. Two new clients."

"That's good. Paying cases?"

"One of them is. What's for dinner?"

"Sea bass with new potatoes and salad."

"Nice. You're so good to me." I gave him a peck on the cheek.

"Wasn't it supposed to be Mrs Crustie's day in today?" he said. "It doesn't look like she's been."

"She won't be cleaning for us anymore."

"Did she resign?"

"Not exactly. I fired her."

"Why would you do that?"

"I caught her having a party in our lounge with some of her friends."

"Are you sure it was a party?"

"Of course I'm sure. They were drinking wine, eating cakes, and singing and dancing. *Our* wine and *our* cakes!"

"Couldn't you have just given her a warning?"

"No, I couldn't. The woman was a liability. We're well shut of her."

"Where will we find another cleaner?"

"We don't need to. I'll do the cleaning."

He laughed. "No, seriously, Jill. Where will we find someone to replace Mrs Crustie?"

"I'm deadly serious. From now on, I'll be doing all the cleaning."

"Good luck with that. I'll give it a week. Two at most."

We were halfway through dinner when Jack suddenly shot up from his chair.

"There's something I want to show you. I left it in my coat pocket." He disappeared into the hallway, and returned a few moments later, clutching a leaflet. "This looks great. We should try it."

"If it's some boring dancing thing, I'm not interested."

"It isn't."

"Or bowling."

"It's paintball. Look." He placed the leaflet on the table in front of me.

"Now you're talking. I'm up for shooting someone with paint. When are we going?"

"By *someone*, I assume you mean *me*?"

"Not necessarily. We should get Kathy and Peter to go with us. We'd annihilate them."

"Good idea. Do you think they'd be up for it?"

"Who cares? Kathy owes me for all the awful things she drags me along to. I'll tell her they have to come."

"I've never seen you so enthusiastic about anything."

"I can't wait to see Kathy plastered with paint. It'll be great."

Chapter 4

The next morning, Jack left early for work. I was still buzzing with thoughts of paintball, so I gave Kathy a call.

"It's me."

"Jill? What's wrong?"

"Nothing."

"Then why are you calling while my brain is still tucked up in bed?"

"We're going paintballing."

"I'm so very pleased for you. Goodbye."

"Wait! I mean *we're* going paintballing. Me and Jack, and you and Peter."

"Is that your way of asking if we'd like to go?"

"It'll be great."

"Actually, I've always fancied having a go at that."

"We'll give you and Peter a good whupping."

"And what are you basing that claim on?" She laughed. "Don't you remember when Dad bought us those toy guns which fired darts with rubber suckers on the ends?"

"No."

"Yes, you do. There was a plastic target included with the set. I hit the bullseye every time; you couldn't even hit the target."

"You've just made that up. I don't remember any of that."

"You must do. Dad confiscated your gun after he caught you firing at my Barbies."

Suddenly, it all came back to me. "You grassed me up."

"You were shooting at my Barbies."

"Are you and Peter up for it, then?"

"Definitely. When did you have in mind?"

"How about this weekend?"

"I'll check with Pete to make sure he doesn't have to work. Can the kids come?"

"It's adults only."

"Okay. I'll see if Pete's mum can take them, and I'll get back to you."

"Great! We're so going to destroy you two."

"In your dreams."

When I stepped out of the door, Megan was in the front garden, watering her plants.

"Megan, thanks for calling me yesterday."

"That's okay. I saw those women leave shortly after you came home. Had they broken in?"

"No. One of them was our cleaner. They were having some kind of party."

"What did you do?"

"I sacked the cleaner and threw them all out."

"I wish I could afford a cleaner."

"They're more trouble than they're worth. I'm going to do it myself from now on."

"Will you have time? You always seem to be really busy."

"I'll have to make time. I suppose I could always resort to magic, if I have to."

She laughed. "Yeah. I guess there's always that option."

"Are you and Ryan still okay?"

"We're getting on great. I've got so much more energy since I started drinking that iron supplement that he introduced me to."

"Are you still drinking it, then?"

"Yeah. I asked Ryan to get a few bottles for me. I have a

drink each morning before I start the day."

"Right. And you feel better for it?"

"Much."

"That's — err — really great."

"Oh no!" Megan pointed up the road. "I'm going inside. Catch you later, Jill."

She'd seen Mr Hosey's train tootling down the road towards us. He pulled up at the end of my driveway, blocking me in.

"Good morning, Jill."

"Morning, Mr Hosey. I was just on my way to work."

"Have you noticed anything?" He pointed to Bessie.

"I don't think so."

"I've removed that hideous face."

"Oh, yes. Of course. She looks much better." Mr Hosey was embroiled in a feud with Mr Kilbride, my neighbour from across the road. Mr Kilbride had painted a face on Mr Hosey's train; Mr Hosey had retaliated by painting a face on Mr Kilbride's house. They were such adults. "Have you two called a truce?"

"Far from it. It's outright war now. Look!" He pointed up the road, and there, steaming towards us was another train, almost identical to Bessie. At the controls was Mr Kilbride.

I watched wide-eyed as this second train came flying past us on the opposite side of the road.

"Sorry, Jill." Mr Hosey jumped back into Bessie. "I can't let him get ahead of me."

I watched, stunned, as the two trains disappeared into the distance.

***

After I'd parked my car in Washbridge, I magicked myself over to Aunt Lucy's house.

"Jill. I'm so glad you're coming with us. I meant to tell you about it yesterday, but with all the rushing around, it totally slipped my mind."

"That's okay. I'm looking forward to it. Are the twins meeting us here?"

"Yes. They should have been here twenty minutes ago, but when were they ever on time? Would you like a drink while we're waiting for them?"

"I'm okay, thanks. I'll just nip upstairs and say hello to Barry and Hamlet."

"Barry is at Dolly's house. She said she'd look after him today."

"Right. I'll just check in with the hamster, then."

Hamlet was in his armchair; he had his earphones in again.

"Hello there!" I waved my hand in front of the cage.

"You again?"

"You were out when I called back yesterday. How was the book fair?"

"Disappointing, but then I find most things are these days."

"Your card payment was rejected."

"The subscription seems to have gone through okay."

"Only because I paid for it using my card."

"That was very generous of you. Thank you very much. But then, I suppose it's only fair recompense for babysitting that hound of yours." He put his earphones back in.

"But—I—err." I was wasting my breath; he was lost on

the high seas with Moby Dick.

The twins arrived as I was on my way down the stairs.

"We're going to the seaside!" they chanted.

"How are we getting there?" I asked.

"The train. It's the best way to travel to the seaside."

"How far away is it?"

"A couple of hours. The weather looks promising. The forecast said it'll be sunny all day."

"Are you ready, girls?" Aunt Lucy appeared.

"Yes!" All three of us shouted.

"Where are you lot off to?"

Oh no! Grandma.

"We're going to Candle Sands, mother." Aunt Lucy stepped forward. "Why don't you come with us? We'd love you to."

The twins and I exchanged a glance. Had Aunt Lucy completely lost her mind?

"It's a bit late to ask me now, Lucy, isn't it? Why didn't you tell me you were going?"

"It was all very last minute. A spur of the moment thing, but there's still time for you to come. You'll enjoy the sea air."

"It must be nice to have the time to go gallivanting off to the seaside. Some of us are too busy to drop everything, and go and build sandcastles. Some of us have more important issues to attend to."

"Never mind. Maybe next time. Come on, girls. We have a train to catch."

"Just a minute." Grandma grabbed my arm, and pulled me to one side. "I need a quick word with Jill."

"What is it, Grandma?"

"Keep an eye open for sand demons," she said in a

whisper.

"Sand — ?"

"Shush. I don't want to scare Lucy and the girls."

"What are sand demons?"

"They're green, and have two heads and large teeth. They're more or less extinct now, but there have been a few tragic incidents over the last few months."

"Tragic? How do you mean?"

"The demons live under the beach—just below the surface. They grab unsuspecting passers-by, and drag them under the sand where they devour them; even the bones."

"That's horrible."

"They're resistant to most spells. Luckily, you're powerful enough to see them off, so just make sure you keep your eyes peeled."

"Okay. Thanks for the warning." I went back to join the others.

"That was close." Amber let out a sigh of relief. "It would have ruined the day if she'd tagged along."

"Why did you tell her that we wanted her to come with us, Mum?" Pearl said.

"Because I knew if I said that, she'd say 'no'. If she'd thought we didn't want her to come with us, she would have invited herself. It's called reverse psychology."

"Brilliant! Well done, Mum."

"Yeah. Well done, Aunt Lucy. You saved the day."

We could have magicked ourselves to Candle Sands, but I'm glad we didn't. The train journey through long stretches of beautiful countryside was delightful. The train was like the old-fashioned ones I'd only ever seen in photographs and movies in the human world. Instead of long, open carriages, there were small compartments which seated only six people. The four of us managed to grab one all to ourselves.

"Can we buy buckets and spades?" Pearl yelled as we walked the short distance from the Candle Sands railway station to the town.

"Yeah! Can we, Mum?" Amber said.

"Remind me how old you two are again?"

"Please, Mum. You have to build sandcastles at the seaside."

"As long as you pay for them yourselves. I paid for the train tickets."

The twins sped off towards the small shop across the road.

"Don't you want a bucket and spade, Jill?"

"No, thanks." I needed my wits about me to keep a look out for sand demons.

"I love this place," Aunt Lucy said. "I used to come here with Grandma and your mother when we were children. It hasn't changed very much since then."

The small town of Candle Sands sat on top of a cliff; in the distance was a white brick lighthouse. A number of paths weaved their way down to the sandy beach below.

"Which one is best, Jill? It's mine, isn't it?" Amber pointed to her sandcastle.

"Rubbish!" Pearl scoffed. "Mine knocks spots off yours, doesn't it, Jill?"

"I'm not acting as the judge." I had no intention of getting involved. "Ask your mum."

Aunt Lucy shot me a look. "I'm not being the judge either. I don't want one of you sulking for the rest of the day. They're both as good as one another."

"But, Mum, mine is much better," Pearl protested.

"Look! Over there!" Aunt Lucy pointed. At first, I thought it was just a clever ploy to distract the twins, but then I realised what she was pointing at. A hundred yards down the beach, a small crowd was gathered around a man and his dog. The small dog was performing tricks, much to the delight of the audience.

"Let's take a closer look." I led the way; Amber and Pearl followed. Aunt Lucy lay back in her deck chair, no doubt appreciative of the peace and quiet.

The dog was small—about the size of a Yorkshire terrier. It was an absolute delight, and seemed to enjoy performing. Its owner, a wizard in his forties, was seated in a deck chair, from where he shouted out one command after another.

"Look!" Amber grabbed my arm. "Behind the deck chair."

I followed her gaze to a small cage in which there were two tiny puppies.

"They're adorable." Pearl led the way over to the cage.

The two pups came over to us, and pushed their tiny paws through the bars of the cage.

The performance had now ended, and the star of the show was enjoying a well-deserved bowl of food. The man in the deck chair leaned over to talk to us. "They're just like their dad, don't you think?"

It was true; the pups were like miniature versions of the performing dog.

"They're gorgeous." Amber was clearly smitten.

"I'm looking for a good home for them, if you're interested?"

"Really?" Pearl said. "How much do you want for them?"

"Hold on, girls." I felt I should step in before they did something rash.

"Five hundred pounds each."

The twins looked at one another, and I knew what was coming.

"We'll take them."

"Wait!" I said. "You need to think about this. It's a big commitment."

"We know what we're doing, Jill," Amber insisted.

That would be a first.

"We don't have enough cash with us," Pearl said. "But we could give you a deposit of a hundred pounds, and then come back with the rest in a couple of days."

"Girls!" I tried again. "Don't you think you should at least talk it over with Aunt Lucy first?"

"Deal." The man shook Pearl's hand. "A hundred pounds now, and the rest when you come to collect them. You've bought yourself two puppies."

The twins whooped with excitement.

"What on earth was going on over there?" Aunt Lucy asked when we were back with her.

"You may well ask." I rolled my eyes. "I'll let the twins explain."

"What will Alan and William say?" Aunt Lucy was horrified at what the twins had done. "Don't you think you should have consulted them first?"

"They'll be fine with it," Amber said.

"Yeah. They both love dogs." Pearl backed up her sister.

Aunt Lucy soon realised that there was no point in arguing with them. They'd made up their minds, and nothing she or I might say would make any difference.

The rest of the day was wonderful. We spent most of the time on the beach, leaving it just long enough to grab lunch in a pretty little café in the town. Fortunately, there was no sign of any sand demons.

"Support the Candle Lighthouse." A wizard with a red collection box was making his way along the beach.

"There you go." Aunt Lucy dropped some coins into the box. The twins and I did the same.

"Is the lighthouse still operational?" I asked.

"Yes. When I'm not trying to drum up contributions, I'm actually the lighthouse keeper."

"Don't you get funds from the authorities?"

"Some, but not enough to keep it going. If it wasn't for the generosity of visitors to the resort, the lighthouse would have closed down years ago. Our candle bill is horrendous."

"Candles?"

"Yes. This is one of only three lighthouses to be powered entirely by candlelight."

"You must get through a lot of them?"

"Thousands, hence the need for the collection. I'm Duncan, by the way. Duncan O'Nuts."

"Nice to meet you, Duncan. I'm Jill. That's Pearl and Amber, and this is my Aunt Lucy."

"We're getting puppies!" Amber blurted out.

"They're so cute." Pearl gushed.

"That's nice for you," Duncan said. "I usually bring my

dog, Bonny, out with me when I'm doing the collection—you'd be surprised how many more donations I get when she's with me."

"Is she poorly?"

"No, but she is very pregnant. In fact, she's due to give birth any day now. You're all welcome to take a tour of the lighthouse if you'd like. I'm just headed back there now."

"We'd love to," Aunt Lucy said. "But we really have to get back home."

"Maybe next time you visit, then."

Chapter 5

Jules was by herself in the office, and quite obviously upset about something.

"What's wrong, Jules?"

"I've had some terrible news about a friend of mine. They say she's gone insane, and she's been locked away in a high security hospital."

"That's terrible. Had she been ill for long?"

"That's just it. I was with Jasmine only a couple of days ago, and she was perfectly fine then. I don't believe what they're saying about her, Jill. I think her mother is behind this."

"How do you mean?"

"Jasmine is a bit wild. She loves a night out and a laugh, but her mother can't handle the fact that Jasmine isn't her *little girl* any longer."

"Even so. It's a bit of a stretch to suggest she'd have her own daughter locked away, just to stop her going out."

"I know, but something's going on. There's no way Jasmine should be locked up. Can you help her, Jill?"

"How do you know Jasmine?"

"We worked together at the black pudding factory. She still works there. Please, Jill, I'm really worried about her."

"Wouldn't it be better if you talked to her mother?"

"Me? No. Her mother hates me, and all of Jasmine's other friends from the factory. She blames us for *corrupting* her daughter."

"Okay. I'll check it out. What's her full name?"

"Jasmine Bold." Jules began to scribble on a sheet of paper. "Her mother's name is Christine. This is her address."

"If I have time, I'll go and talk to her later today."

"Thanks, Jill. I really appreciate it."

I started towards my office door.

"Jill?"

"Yeah?"

"Why are you covered in sand?"

Oh bum! "I—err—fell into the sandpit."

"You have a sandpit?"

"Yeah. We had it put in recently for when Kathy's kids come over. I was in the garden this morning, and I tripped and fell into it."

"Oh? Right." Jules looked confused, and who could blame her?

"Sandpit? Is that the best you could come up with?" Winky shook his head.

"You shouldn't be listening."

"Why not? I've got nothing better to do. Where have you really been?"

"If you must know, I went to the seaside."

"It's nice for some. Why didn't you tell gorgeous, out there, the truth?"

"Because she would have asked where I went, and I could hardly tell her I've been to Candle Sands in the sup world, could I?"

"And yet, you're telling your cat."

"I don't know why. It's not like I have to report to you."

"How come I didn't get to go to the seaside?"

"Cats don't like water."

"I could have relaxed in a deck chair and soaked up the sun."

"You can't travel to Candlefield. You're not a sup."

"How do you know? How can you be sure I'm not really a shape-shifter? Maybe I'm really some sad, old geezer who just turns into a cat whenever you're around."

"That's ridiculous. I'd know if you were." I hesitated. "You aren't, are you?"

"That's for me to know, and for you to fret about. Anyway, where is it?"

"Where's what?"

"My stick of rock, of course. You may have left me here all alone while you were at the seaside, but even you wouldn't have been heartless enough not to have brought me back a stick of rock."

"Rock? I — err — how about some salmon?"

"Red, not pink?"

"Obviously."

I watched Winky as he gobbled down the salmon. He'd obviously been joking about the old man; I'd know if he was a shape-shifter.

Wouldn't I?

"Have you checked if you've had any more quotes?" He licked his lips, and jumped onto my desk.

"Yuk, you stink of salmon."

"It smells better than that perfume you wear. So? Have you had any more quotes for decorating the office?"

I'd actually forgotten all about that, but when I logged in to check, there were five more quotes waiting for me.

"They're all too expensive. This one is even higher than the ones I got yesterday."

"What about that one at the bottom of the list?" He pointed with his paw. "That looks a reasonable price."

"Dectastic? What kind of name is that for a company?"

"Never mind their name. Look at the price."

Dectastic's quote was just under half the next lowest, and even better, they'd said they could do the job immediately.

"That seems too good to be true."

"You don't want to pay the higher prices, but you're wary of the lower price. You can't have it both ways. What kind of reviews do they have?"

I clicked on the link to the company's profile. "Very good, actually. An average of four-point four out of five."

"There you go, then."

"I don't understand how they can quote such a low price?"

"Maybe they've had a cancellation, and need to fill the gap? Who knows? But if you hesitate, they may get another job, and then you'll be stuck with the higher prices."

"Do you think so?"

"I'm positive."

"Okay, then, I'll do it." I was just about to click on the button to place the order when I spotted a note included with their bid. "Hold on. It says that the quote is for carrying out the work during the night. That's a bit weird, isn't it?"

"Not necessarily. Maybe they work twenty-four seven. I imagine some customers prefer the work to be done overnight. That way there's much less disruption."

"I guess you're right. It would mean we wouldn't have to close down the office while they do the work."

"There you go then. What are you waiting for?"

"Okay." I clicked on the button. "All done!"

Thirty minutes later, Kathy showed up unannounced; she caught me sharpening my pencils.

"I can see you're busy." She grinned.

"I hate blunt pencils."

"How many pencils do you have?"

"Thirty-one. One for each day of the month."

"Can't you use the same one on more than one day?"

"No because then it would be blunt."

"You could sharpen it."

"I prefer to have just the one pencil-sharpening day per month. It's more efficient."

"And I take it that today is—?"

"Pencil sharpening day? Yes. Anyway, how come you aren't at work? Have you got the day off?"

"Kind of, but not through choice."

"What happened?"

"I had a call from your grandmother last night, to say she doesn't need me, Chloe or Maria to go in, and when I walked past the shop just now it was all boarded up."

"What? Has it closed down?"

"There's nothing to say so, and that's not the impression your grandmother gave me on the phone. She said she'd be in touch in a few days."

"Do you think it has something to do with Yarnstormers opening?"

"Could be. Your guess is as good as mine."

"How has she taken the whole Yarnstormers thing?"

"Remarkably well. I expected her to go ballistic, but she hasn't mentioned them once. It's all a little unnerving. Do you think you can find out what she's up to?"

"I can try, but I doubt I'll have any more success than you would."

Just then, Jules came through with a tray of tea and biscuits.

"Thanks, Jules." Kathy took one of the cups and two biscuits. "I asked her to make us a drink, I hope you don't mind?"

"Of course not. Make yourself at home. You usually do."

Jules handed me my cup of tea, and then turned to Kathy. "How do the kids like the sandpit?"

"Which sandpit?" Kathy looked confused.

"The one at Jill's house."

"Jill?" Kathy turned to me.

"I—err—Jules has rather let the cat out of the bag. I've had a sandpit put in the back garden. I thought it would be nice for the kids to play in when they come over."

"Sorry, Jill," Jules said. "I didn't realise it was a secret."

"That's okay. Thanks for the drinks."

"You've had a sandpit put in?" Kathy was open-mouthed.

I nodded.

"For the kids?"

I nodded again.

"But you don't even like them coming over to your place."

"That isn't true."

"When was the last time you had them over?"

"I—err—I don't keep track."

"Have you really had a sandpit put in for them?"

"Err—yes, but maybe it wasn't such a good idea? They might trip and fall into it. I probably should take it out."

"Don't do that. A sandpit is a great idea, and a lovely gesture. Maybe I misjudged you after all. Just wait until I tell the kids. They'll be thrilled."

"Great."

"Talking of the kids. Pete's mum has said she'll have them on Saturday, so we're good for paintball."

"Nice one. Prepare to be annihilated."

"Dream on."

As soon as Kathy had left, Winky came out from under the sofa. "Watching you is like watching a train wreck in slow motion."

"Be quiet."

"You just don't know when to stop digging, do you?" He was rolling across the floor, laughing. "Sandpit? Priceless!"

"Shut up." I grabbed the Yellow Pages. "What would sandpit suppliers come under?"

After Kathy had left, Jules came through to collect the empty cups. "Sorry about the sandpit thing, Jill. I honestly didn't realise it was meant to be a surprise."

"It's okay. I should have said."

Just then the outer door crashed open.

"It sounds like we have a visitor. Am I expecting anyone, Jules?"

"Not as far as I know. I'll go and see who it is." Moments later, she was back. "It's that policeman, Detective Riley. He insists on seeing you straightaway."

"You'd better show him in."

"Shall I make him a drink?"

"No. I don't want to waste a good teabag on him."

"You can go through, Detective." Jules held the door open for him.

He brushed past her without so much as a thank you.

"Hello, Leo."

"It's Detective, to you."

"Sorry. Hello, Detective Leo."

He scowled. "You think you're funny, don't you?"

"I have my moments. How are your hands?"

"Hands?"

"I thought they might still be sore after the whupping we gave you in the tug-of-war."

"I don't have time for your idle chit-chat. I'm here because there have been reports that you are keeping an animal on these premises."

"I did have a kangaroo in here earlier, but it had to skip town."

"Do you or do you not have a cat in here?"

Fortunately, Winky was back under the sofa, out of sight.

"What business is that of the police? The terms of my lease are a matter between me and my landlord. I fail to see what business it is of yours."

He began to walk around the room, so I quickly cast the 'hide' spell to make Winky invisible.

"What are these?" Riley was pointing at the waste bin.

"What are what?"

"All of these empty salmon cans?"

"I like fish. So, sue me."

"I believe you are hiding a cat in here somewhere."

"You're right. It's in here." I pulled open the top drawer. "Here it is. Catch." I threw him the mini-Winky toy.

"Very funny." He dropped it into the bin.

"There is no good reason for you to be here, so unless

you have a warrant to search these premises, I'd like you to leave now."

"I'm going, but you haven't heard the last of this."

With that, he left, slamming the door behind him.

"What's eating him?" Winky said.

I almost jumped out of my skin because he was still invisible, and I hadn't realised he'd jumped onto my desk.

I quickly reversed the 'hide' spell.

"He was checking if I had any animals in here."

"Is there so little crime in Washbridge that the police have nothing better to do?"

"It's not that. He's up to something, and I intend to find out what it is."

Chapter 6

I didn't call ahead because I was fairly sure Jasmine Bold's mother would have refused to see me.

When she answered the door, I could tell she'd been crying.

"Yes?"

"Mrs Christine Bold? I'm Jill Gooder."

"What do you want? I never buy at the door."

"I'm not selling anything. I'm a friend of your daughter."

"I've never heard her mention your name. How do you know Jasmine?"

"I work at the black pudding factory; I haven't been there long. I was just wondering if she's alright?"

"Of course she isn't alright. That's why they've locked her up."

"She seemed okay the other day at work."

"She was, but then she wasn't. She changed just like that. I've never seen anything quite like it. She scared me."

"Do you have any idea what might have caused it?"

"I blame that boyfriend of hers."

"Jasmine has a boyfriend? She's never mentioned him."

"She only met him very recently. That's why I think he must be responsible. Probably gave her drugs or something."

"Do you know his name?"

"Billy Bhoy. I knew as soon as I saw him that he was bad news. All those tattoos and piercings, and his shaved head. I tried to warn Jasmine, but would she listen? No. She never does." At that, Mrs Bold broke down in tears.

"I'd better be going. Sorry to have upset you. Tell

Jasmine I hope she gets better soon."

Jules had been convinced that Jasmine's mother had somehow had her daughter locked up for no good reason. Even though I'd spent no more than a few minutes with Christine Bold, I was convinced that wasn't the case. The woman's distress had seemed genuine, and I was now far more interested in talking to the boyfriend. His looks might have disturbed Christine Bold, but that wasn't what worried me. I was far more concerned that he and Jasmine had only recently got together, which in my book made him someone I needed to talk to.

***

Back in Washbridge, I thought I should check out what was happening at Ever. Even though Kathy had warned me, I was still shocked to find the shop boarded up.

What was Grandma up to? She surely hadn't thrown in the towel just because Yarnstormers had opened up across the road. She was many things, but a quitter wasn't one of them. I tried her phone, but got only her recorded message: *Mirabel here. I'm too busy to talk to you. Don't bother to leave a message because I can't be bothered to check them.*

"That was even easier than I expected," a familiar voice said.

I turned around to find Ma Chivers standing there; she had a huge grin on her face.

"What are you talking about, Ma?"

"I thought your grandmother would have put up more of a fight. I guess I over-estimated her."

"I wouldn't go counting your chickens just yet."

"Really?" She gestured towards the boarded-up shop. "Looks like she's given up to me. As you know, I'm not a vindictive woman. There's still a job for your sister at Yarnstormers, if she wants it."

"Kathy doesn't need your job. She already has one."

"Hmm? We'll see. Well, I'd better get back. It looks like we have a queue again."

I had no intention of admitting it to Ma Chivers, but I was worried. Maybe, Grandma had had enough. If so, Kathy might just have to take Ma Chivers' job after all.

If only I could locate Grandma. Maybe Aunt Lucy knew where she was. I gave her a call.

"Sorry, Jill. I haven't seen her today. Is it something I can help with?"

"No, not really, but there was something else I wanted to ask you."

"Yes?"

"I had to fire my cleaner."

"Wasn't she up to the job?"

"Her work was okay, but only because she used magic. She was having a laugh at my expense. The final straw was when I caught her having a shindig in our lounge with some of her friends. They were drinking my wine, and eating my chocolates."

"The cheek of some people."

"Tell me about it."

"I assume you're on the lookout for another cleaner, then?"

"No. I'm done with cleaners. I'm going to do it myself from now on."

"You? Do the cleaning?"

Why did everyone sound so shocked when I said that?

"I'm going to use magic."

"That could be dangerous. You mustn't let anyone catch you."

"If Agatha Crustie can get away with it, I don't see why I can't. I just need to find a way to do it while I'm away from the house. That's what I wanted to ask you about."

"You need a 'schedule' spell."

"I don't think I've come across those."

"They're a little complicated, but nothing you won't be able to master. I have details of one upstairs somewhere, but it might take me a few minutes to put my hands on it."

"No problem. I'll pick it up next time I'm over there."

***

As soon as I arrived home, Jack called to me from the lounge.

"You're home early." I gave him a peck on the cheek.

"I was working out this way, so I decided to call it a day rather than drive all the way back to West Chipping."

"Now I'm home, you might as well make a start on dinner."

"Oh no you don't. It's your turn."

"Is it? Oh, yeah. Of course."

"Is there something you forgot to tell me, Jill?"

"I don't think so."

"Are you sure?"

"What are you talking about?"

"A sandpit, for example?"

"Oh? Right. Yeah."

"When I got home, there were three men digging up the back garden."

"Didn't I mention that?"

"You know you didn't."

"Did you send them away?"

"I was going to until they explained that you'd placed the order earlier today. They said you'd even paid a premium for an *expedited* installation. That's their white van parked across the road."

"Right. You're probably wondering why I ordered a sandpit."

"Yep."

"I got to thinking about Mikey and Lizzie. Whenever they come over here, there isn't much for them to do."

"They never come over here. You've always said they're too noisy, and they make a mess."

"I'm sure I never said that."

"Why the sudden change of heart?"

"I just thought it would be nice for them."

"It is. I'd love to have them over here more often, but why the need for the expedited installation?"

"I think that must be a mistake. I just told them to do it as soon as possible."

"According to the guy I spoke to, the expedited service costs an extra hundred pounds."

"Really? Oh well, what's done is done. I suppose I'd better make a start on dinner."

"Before you do, something arrived for you today."

"For me? Where is it?"

"I put it in the bedroom."

"What is it?"

"You'll see."

A parcel for me. How exciting! I hurried up the stairs.

"Jack! Get this giant triangle out of here!"

Before starting dinner, I offered the workmen, who were still busy on the sandpit, twenty pounds to take the giant triangle away in their van.

"What do you want us to do with it, Mrs?" the man with the goatee asked.

"Take it home to your kids, burn it, take it to the dump— I don't care. Just as long as you get it out of my sight."

Over dinner, I told Jack about the visit from Leo Riley.

"Please tell me you're joking." Jack looked horrified.

"I wish I was. He turned up unannounced, and started interrogating me about keeping a cat on the premises."

"That's ridiculous. Unless you're keeping a dangerous animal in there, it's no concern of the police. Do you want me to have a word with him?"

"No. I've told you before that I can fight my own battles. Leo Riley doesn't scare me."

"Just don't do anything stupid. He might be trying to provoke you into doing something that *is* an arrestable offence."

"Don't worry. When I murder him, I won't leave any clues."

***

"What time will you get back?" Jack asked as I was leaving the house. I was going to Chez Piper to work under cover.

"I doubt I'll be back before midnight, so please try to be quiet in the morning. I'm going to have a lie-in."

"I'll be as quiet as a mouse." He gave me a kiss. "Just be careful tonight."

Chez Piper was located close to the turn-off to Candlefield—not that the Pipers or any other humans would have been aware of that because the road was visible only to sups. I could still remember the problems I'd encountered the first time I'd tried to drive there for my mother's funeral. That seemed like a thousand years ago now.

"What do you want me to do?" I asked Mrs Piper. We were in the office, which was located at the side of the restaurant.

"The food is going missing from the storage room, so you'll need to be based in the kitchen."

"Perhaps I could help to prepare the meals?"

"I don't think so. Our standards are very high. No offence."

"What then?"

"You can do the washing up."

"You mean load and unload the dishwasher?"

"Normally, that's what it would entail, but our dishwasher isn't working at the moment, so they'll all have to be washed by hand." She pointed to a huge pile of dirty pots and pans.

"I thought the restaurant only opened a few minutes ago?"

"It did. Those are left over from lunchtime. You'll need to get cracking, otherwise we'll run out of crockery." She handed me a white overall, and left me to it.

"Hi!" A young man, with eyebrows so thick they probably had their own postcode, came over to talk to me. "I'm Tigh Howe. I'm the sous chef."

"Nice to meet you. I'm Jill. Trust me to start here on the day that the dishwasher broke."

"It's been broken for a few days. The Pipers are usually good at getting that kind of thing sorted quickly, but they seem to have been distracted for the last few days."

The pace was relentless. I was still at it an hour after the restaurant had closed, and all the other staff had left. I had a thumping headache, my back was killing me, and my fingers looked like prunes.

I found both Mr and Mrs Piper in the office.

"Jill. How did it go?"

"Alright, but you really need to get the dishwasher mended."

"I meant the pilferage. Did you spot anything?"

"Not a thing, and I was standing right next to the storage area. If anything had been taken, I would have seen it. Are you absolutely sure you want to continue with this? As I mentioned when you came to my office, my charges will be more than the cost of the food being stolen. You'd be better off spending the money on getting the dishwasher repaired."

"It's very important we get to the bottom of this. We'd like you to carry on for at least a few more days. Same time tomorrow?"

"Okay, but please get the dishwasher fixed."

***

On my way back home, I decided to drop in at my offices. Dectastic had promised they would get most of the decorating completed that night, and would return the following night to finish off. I was looking forward to seeing what the place looked like with a lick of paint—goodness knows it was long overdue.

As I walked up the stairs, I could hear sounds coming from the outer office. That was a good sign—they were obviously already hard at it.

"What the—?"

I looked around in disbelief. There were three of them working in there. Three cats, that is! One was on a stepladder, painting the ceiling; one was painting the far wall, and the third was painting the skirting board.

"What's going on?" I yelled.

The tabby on the ladder almost lost his balance.

"Who are you?" the Siamese painting the wall said.

"What do you think you're doing?"

"What's it got to do with you?"

"This is my office. And what colour is that supposed to be?"

He glanced down at the tin. "Blue."

"What shade of blue?"

He shrugged. "Navy, I guess."

"You guess? This room is meant to be sky blue. Look at all of these streaks. And where are your dust covers? Look at the state of that desk!"

Mrs V's desk had splashes of paint all over it.

"Who's in charge here?"

"The boss is next door." The Siamese pointed.

"Is he? I'd better have a word with him then."

I found a similar scene in my office where three more

cats were hard at work. The walls were streaky, and there wasn't a single dust cover to be seen. Meanwhile, fast asleep on my desk, was Winky.

I walked over, and slapped the desk. Winky jumped so hard he tumbled onto the floor.

"Hey! Do you mind? I could have broken my leg."

"I'll break more than your leg when I get hold of you."

"What's wrong?"

I could barely speak because I was hyper-ventilating. "You're Dectastic, aren't you?"

"None other. What do you think of it so far?"

"For a start, the paint is the wrong colour."

"It looks about right to me."

"About right? This room is supposed to be magnolia, but it's brown. And the walls out there are supposed to be sky blue, not navy."

"I doubt anyone would notice."

"The walls are streaky, and the paint has splashed all over the floor and furniture. How could you let them do this?"

"It isn't my fault. Jason said he knew a few lads who had done some decorating."

"Who's Jason?"

"The Siamese out front."

"Why didn't you at least supervise?"

"I had intended to, but I guess I must have fallen asleep."

"What are you going to do about this mess? I want these comedians out of here right now."

"But they haven't finished."

"Yes, they have!"

Chapter 7

The next morning, I didn't wake until just after nine o'clock. I would have slept even longer had it not been for the deafening crash that came from out on the street. Somehow, I managed to drag my tired body out of bed, and over to the window to check what was going on.

A few yards up the road from my house was a scene of devastation. The trains belonging to Mr Hosey and Mr Kilbride had collided, and both engines were lying on their sides, blocking half of the road. A number of neighbours were already out on the street, trying to make sense of what they were seeing. It was obvious that neither of the train drivers had been badly hurt in the collision because they were standing in the middle of the road, exchanging insults with one another.

Jack had already gone to work, but had left a note for me on the bedside table:

Have a safe day, sleeping beauty. See you tonight. Love Jack xxx

After I'd showered and dressed, I went downstairs for breakfast.

That's when I saw it!

What the—? The sandpit was huge! It had been dark when I'd got in the previous evening, so this was the first time I'd actually seen the finished article. There was barely any lawn left.

I went outside, bowl of cornflakes in hand, to take a closer look. I couldn't fault the construction, but it was large enough to accommodate a class full of kids. What had I been thinking? I hadn't—that was the problem.

Winky had been right as usual, I'd started digging myself into a hole, and ended up with a ginormous sandpit. Kathy and the kids had better appreciate it.

When I turned back to the house, I almost jumped out of my skin, as I came face to face with two man-sized frogs. Instinctively, I went into self-defence mode, and was about to shrink them when I remembered what had happened with the giant ants.

"Tony? Clare?"

"Morning, Jill." Tony's voice came from the taller of the two frogs.

"What do you think of these?" said Clare, the smaller frog.

"They're—err—very good. I take it you have another cosplay event?"

"Yes, this Saturday."

"Let me guess. FrogCon?"

"Frog?" Clare said. "No. Why would there be a Con for frogs?"

"That would be a bit weird." Tony laughed.

"So, what are the costumes for?"

"ToadCon, of course."

"Obviously. Silly me."

"We have spare tickets if you and Jack would like to join us."

"We'd love to, but we've already arranged to go paintballing with my sister and her husband."

"Paintballing?" Tony shook his toad head. "Oh dear."

"Oh dear." Clare echoed.

"What's wrong with paintball?"

"Nothing. I'm sure it will be fine." Tony sounded less than convincing. "It's just that we went once, and our friend, Frank, ended up with a broken nose and two black eyes."

"I thought it was safe."

"It is usually, but Frank is very fussy about his hair. He refused to wear the helmet and goggles."

"Was he okay?"

"His hair was fine, but it took a couple of weeks for the bruising to disappear."

"We'll be sure to wear all of the safety equipment." I assured them. "I suppose I'd better get going. I'm already running late."

"Be careful when you pull off your driveway, Jill. I assume you've seen the carnage on the road."

"I certainly have."

"We saw the collision, didn't we, Clare? Both trains were trying to move to the opposite side of the road, and neither would give way to the other. Then 'smash'. They were both on their sides. With a bit of luck, it will put both trains out of action for a while. It's positively dangerous setting foot onto the pavement these days."

When I left for work, the trains were still on their sides, and Hosey and Kilbride were still going at it hammer and tongs. I was determined not to get involved, so I kept my head down until I was in the car, and then I managed to slip slowly past the wreckage by mounting the pavement.

**

Mrs V did not look impressed.

"I'm not impressed, Jill."

See? What did I tell you?

"Morning, Mrs V."

"What kind of cowboy outfit did you get to do the decorating?"

"I was going to talk to you about that."

"Look at these desks, and the floor. They're covered in paint."

"Yeah, like I said, I—"

"And what colour do you call this? It isn't sky blue, that's for sure. It looks more like midnight blue to me."

"It's actually Navy, but—"

"And look at all these streaks. Is your office any better?"

"Not really, but don't worry. I'm going to get someone in to put all of this right."

"When?"

"Soon. Very soon. I promise."

"I would hope so, dear. I'm just glad I hadn't left my knitting out on the desk."

My office didn't look any better than it had the night before. In fact, it looked much worse. The culprit was nowhere to be seen.

"Where are you, Winky?"

"I'm not here." The voice came from under the sofa.

"Come out here, now."

He crept out, but didn't make (one-eyed) eye contact. "It doesn't look so bad in the daylight, does it?"

"You are joking, I assume? Look at the state of this place. There are paint splashes everywhere. And what colour do you call this?"

"Magnolia. Ish."

"There's no 'ish' about it. This is brown. And look at all these streaks. What were you thinking, Winky?"

"I was trying to do you a favour. I was trying to save you money."

"Oh, I get it. This was all done out of the goodness of your heart?"

"Exactly." He looked up for the first time. "That's the kind of guy I am."

"What was your cut?"

"What do you mean?"

"How much of the payment were you getting?"

"Not much."

"How much?"

"Fifty per cent."

"I want my money back, and I expect it to be on my desk by the end of the day, or you'd better start looking for somewhere else to live."

"I'm as much a victim in all this as you," he pleaded.

"And how do you work that out?"

"Jason promised me that he knew what he was doing. He lied to me."

"That's not my problem."

"I may have a way out of this."

"I'm listening."

"I've found someone else who will come in and sort it all out."

"Who's that?"

"His name is Grayson. He's Jason's brother."

"No chance!"

"But Grayson really does know his stuff."

"I don't want Jason, Grayson, Mason or any other feline decorator with a rhyming name in these offices. I'll find someone to sort out this mess. Just make sure you get my money back to me before the end of business today."

"Will an I.O.U. do?"

"Cash in full. Or get your suitcase packed!"

***

It was almost lunchtime when Mrs V came through to my office. She did a double-take at the state of the walls, sighed deeply, and then said, "Madeline's mother and a man are here. They would like a word if you can spare them a few minutes."

"Sure. Send them in."

Mrs V glanced again at the walls. "Magnolia my bottom."

I wouldn't have thought it possible that Deli could find a shorter skirt than those I'd seen her wear previously, but somehow, she'd managed it. Either every mirror in their house was broken, or she needed a crash course in how to apply lipstick.

Not that I was judging. Obviously.

"Jill." She gave me a hug. "Thanks for seeing us like this."

"No problem."

"We were in town to buy some tripe, weren't we, Nails?"

He stopped biting his thumb nail just long enough to nod. As he did, I noticed that he was sporting a pair of bottle-top cufflinks.

Nice.

"Nails is very fussy about his tripe. We have to get it from that stall in the market. You've probably seen it: 'Tripe and Stuff'?"

"I'm not really a big fan of tripe."

"Me neither, Jill. Turns my stomach just to look at it, but Nails can't get enough of it, can you, Sugarchops?"

He managed another nod.

Deli glanced around the room. "You've redecorated, I see."

"Bit of a disaster, I'm afraid."

"Who did you get to do it?"

"I—err—you wouldn't have heard of them. I'm going to have to get someone else in to redo it all. It's the wrong colour and there are streaks everywhere."

"Nails will do it for you, won't you, Sugarchops?"

"Nails?" I was horrified at the thought. "Err—that's very kind, but I really need to get the professionals in to sort this lot out."

"Nails is a professional. He did his apprenticeship and everything. Even got a certificate, haven't you?"

"Certificate, yeah." He nodded, as he continued to bite his nails.

"I don't know. I kind of need it doing straightaway."

"No problem. Nails can start later today, can't you? He'll have this place looking good as new in no time."

"What would it cost?"

"We wouldn't charge you anything, Jill. You're like family. Just the cost of the materials—that's all."

"I couldn't possibly let you do it for free."

"You have no choice. Like I said, I think of you as a second daughter. What colours did you have in mind?"

"Magnolia in here and sky blue in the outer office."

"Did you get that, Nails?"

He nodded again. Nodding seemed to be his speciality.

"Thank you. That's very kind."

"Our pleasure, Jill. Well, I suppose we'd better get the

tripe home."

"Didn't you call to see me about something?"

"Oh yes. I'd forget my leg if it wasn't screwed on. I wanted a quick word about Madeline."

"Is she okay?"

"Yeah, she's fine, but I overheard her on the phone the other day. I reckon she's thinking of moving back to London. Has she said anything to you about that?"

"London? No." I lied.

"I'd hate for her to move away again. She and Nails are just starting to get along, aren't you, Sugarchops?" She didn't wait for the obligatory nod. "Will you have a word with her, Jill? If she is thinking of leaving, will you try to change her mind? She listens to you."

"Sure. I'll mention it the next time I see her."

"Thanks, Jill. You're a sapphire." Deli stood up. "Come on, Nails. I'll take the tripe home while you go and buy the paint." She turned to me. "He'll see you later today."

"Great. Thanks."

As soon as they were out of the door, Winky jumped onto my desk.

"You're going to trust *that guy* to decorate the office?"

"He can't do any worse than Grayson has already done."

"Jason."

"Whatever. Nails has a certificate and everything."

"A certificate?" He rolled his eye. "For what? Nail biting?"

***

Billy Bhoy lived in a small bedsit in one of the rougher parts of Washbridge. Not only was he covered in tattoos and piercings, but he was built like the proverbial brick you-know-what house.

I could see why he wouldn't have been Christine Bold's first choice as a boyfriend for her daughter.

"Can I help you?" His soft, polite tone took me by surprise.

"My name is Jill Gooder. I wonder if I could speak to you about Jasmine Bold?"

"How do you know Jasmine?"

"I work with her at the black pudding factory. We're all very worried about her."

"Me too. Do come in." He led the way into the cutest little lounge. The matching sofa and armchair were a very pleasing floral pattern, which complemented the wallpaper. There were lace doilies on the small coffee table.

"Can I get you a drink? Coffee? Tea? I have Earl Grey."

"Thanks, but no. I'm okay."

"Have a seat, at least." He pointed to the sofa.

"All the girls at the factory are worried about Jasmine," I said. "Do you have any news?"

"Nothing. The first I knew about it was when I called around to see her. Her mother said she'd gone crazy, and had been locked up in a high security hospital. I didn't believe her at first. Jasmine's mother doesn't like me; she wanted Jasmine to dump me."

"Do you know why she doesn't like you?"

"Why do you think?" He pointed to the tattoos on his arms, and then patted his shaved head. "I scare some people."

"How was Jasmine the last time you saw her?"

"Fine. She was very happy. We only met recently, but we really hit it off. I want to go and see her, but the hospital won't let me in."

"You've tried?"

"Of course, but they're only allowing relatives in. I'm really worried about her."

"If I ask you something, will you promise not to be offended or angry?"

"Okay?"

"Do you do drugs of any kind?"

"No!" he said, without hesitation. "I have never, and would never touch any kind of drug. I don't even smoke or drink. Is that what Jasmine's mother thinks? That I gave her drugs?" He shook his head, and I could see he was fighting back the tears. "I'd never do anything to hurt Jasmine."

"I'm sorry if I've upset you."

"It doesn't matter about me. I just want Jasmine to be okay."

"We all do." I stood up. "Thanks for talking to me."

"Will you let me know if you hear anything?"

I promised I would, and then left. Whatever had caused Jasmine's sudden decline into madness, I was quite confident that Billy Bhoy had played no part in it.

I needed to see Jasmine for myself, and I needed to do it alone.

Chapter 8

I thought I'd better warn Mad that her mother had found out she was thinking of moving away from Washbridge.

We'd arranged to meet in Spooky Wooky.

"Blueberry muffin, Jill?" Larry greeted me.

"No, thanks. I've given them up."

"Really?"

"Of course not. I'll have a caramel latte too, please."

"Mad's over by the window. I'll bring your order over, if you like?"

"Please, but I need to pay first."

"Mad has already paid for these. She knew what you'd be having."

"Oh? Okay, thanks."

Mad was staring out of the window, and hadn't noticed me come in.

"Thanks for the drink and muffin, Mad."

"Sorry, Jill. I was miles away. What's all this about Mum coming to see you?"

"You have to promise you won't mention I told you any of this."

"Okay."

"She knows you're thinking of leaving Washbridge."

"Oh bum!"

Hey, that's my catchphrase.

"Apparently, she heard you on the phone."

"I'm so stupid! I should never have made those calls from her house. What did she say?"

"That she didn't want you to leave. She seemed quite upset. She wants me to try to talk you out of it."

"You'd be wasting your breath. I've made up my mind. I can't wait to get away from Washbridge."

"I figured as much, but I thought I owed it to Deli to at least mention it to you. Especially now that Nails has agreed to redecorate my offices."

"He did? How did you persuade him to do that?"

"I didn't. Your mother told him he had to do it. I'll be honest with you, I'm a bit worried about it. Does he know what he's doing?"

"You should be okay. From what I can make out, he's actually very good at it, but he's too lazy to find any work."

"Your mum insisted that I only pay for the materials."

"Good for you. By the way, have you been doing much work for Constance Bowler?"

"Not much so far. I did help her to catch some thieves who were stealing garden equipment from GT, and selling it in the human world. They tried to steal a couple of gnomes from my mother's house."

"I didn't realise your mother was into garden gnomes."

"It's more Alberto's thing. He has a garden full of them."

"Oh dear."

"You haven't heard the best of it. They all have names."

"How very sad."

A few minutes later, Mad had to shoot off because she was due back at the library. I was just about to leave too when someone called my name.

"You're Jill Gooder, aren't you?" The woman was wearing red dungarees and green galoshes.

"That's right."

"I thought so. I saw the article about you in Ghost Times."

"Oh? I wasn't aware they'd run one."

"It was a short profile on you. The first sup to be able to travel between GT and the human and sup worlds. It's an honour to meet you."

"Thank you very much, err—?"

"Karen. Karen Coombes. I'll be honest; the reason I came in here today was that I was hoping to run into you. The article mentioned that you had a blueberry muffin obsession, and Spooky Wooky sell the best muffins in GT."

Sheesh. Of all the things to be known for.

"How can I help?"

"It's a little embarrassing. Could we speak outside?"

"Of course."

She led the way out of the shop, and into the small alleyway at the side of the building.

"I've been cheated out of money owing to me. Wages that I earned working for a company called Hauntings Unlimited."

"How did that happen?"

"It isn't just me. There are lots of us in the same boat. If I can get some of the others together, would you be prepared to meet with us? That would help you to get a better picture of what's happening."

"Sure. I'd be happy to. I'll give you my phone number. Give me a call when you've managed to talk to the others and arrange something."

"Thanks, Jill. That's great."

***

Much to my surprise, Nails was already hard at work when I arrived back at the office. Even more encouraging was that he appeared to be making a good job of it.

For some reason, Mrs V was sporting one of her knitted hats.

"Everything okay, Mrs V?"

"Fine, dear, thanks."

"Why are you wearing the hat?"

"Can we speak in your office?"

"Sure." I led the way next door.

"I've just realised why you're wearing it," I said. "I suppose the hat is in case of paint splashes?"

"No, it's not that. This man seems to know what he's doing, and he's put dust sheets over the furniture."

"So why the hat, then?"

"It's to protect myself from the flying fingernails. I've already been hit on the head with them twice, so I decided I needed some protection."

"I see. How does he manage to bite his nails and paint at the same time?"

"I don't know. It's quite an art. Oh, and while you were out, that horrible policeman came around again. He wanted to look in your office, but I told him that he'd have to get a warrant to get past me. I stood in front of your office door, and dared him to lay a hand on me."

"That was very brave of you. Thank you."

"What is he looking for, Jill?"

"Evidence that I'm keeping an animal in here."

"Why would he concern himself with something like that? Surely he has bigger fish to fry?"

"I don't know, but I intend to find out."

As soon as Mrs V had gone back to her desk, I called Winky out from under the sofa.

"Would you like to redeem yourself?"

"For what?"

"The mess your so-called decorator friends have made of my office."

"I've already refunded your payment." He pointed. "The cash is on your desk."

"That only goes part of the way to making up for the inconvenience you've caused me."

"What else do you want me to do?"

"This is for your benefit too. I want you to get your gang to follow Detective Riley. He has suddenly taken an unhealthy interest in whether or not I'm keeping an animal on the premises."

"What's it worth?"

"I'm not paying you. Apart from the fact that you already owe me one anyway, this is in your interest too. If I can't get him off my back, he's sure to discover that you live here sooner or later. Then it will be out on the streets for you."

"Okay. I'll get my guys on it."

"Good man."

Kathy phoned.

"I've just had a call from your grandmother. She wants me, Chloe and Maria to report for work in the morning."

"What's going on with Ever?"

"I have no idea. I was hoping you could tell me."

"I'm as much in the dark as you are. I've tried to get hold of her a few times, but she seems to have gone to ground. I was beginning to think she might have decided to shut up shop for good."

"It doesn't sound like it, thank goodness. Pete's business is doing well, but I still wouldn't want to lose my wage."

"I take it you and Peter are still on for paintball on Saturday?"

"You bet. We've been practising with Mikey's water guns."

"That's cheating."

"All's fair in love and paintball. Oh, and I've told the kids about the sandpit. Lizzie is thrilled, but Mikey says he's too old for them now. Is it still okay for us to come over this Sunday?"

"I suppose so. Look, I'd better get going. I'm really busy."

"Let me know if you hear from your grandmother."

"Will do."

I'd no sooner ended the call with Kathy than my phone rang again. It was Petra Piper.

"Mrs Piper? Have you changed your mind about wanting me to come over there tonight?" I really wasn't looking forward to another shift of dishwashing.

"Some more food has gone missing overnight."

"How can that be? Nothing was taken while I was there."

"It must have happened later. After the restaurant closed."

"Do you have CCTV inside the restaurant?"

"Yes, but it only covers a few areas. Peter has just spent the last hour watching it. There's nothing suspicious on there. Nothing at all."

"Based on what you've just told me, there doesn't seem to be any point in my being there while the restaurant is open. Whatever is happening is obviously taking place later. Why don't I come over just before the restaurant closes? I'll stay there overnight, and see if I can get to the bottom of this once and for all."

"Do you mind doing that?"

"Not at all. It's all part of the service." Anything was better than spending another night pot washing. "I'll see you tonight."

***

Now that I'd fired Agatha Crustie, I needed to sort out the spells that would ensure our house was kept clean and tidy. Aunt Lucy had said I needed to use a 'schedule' spell, and had promised to look one out for me.

When I arrived at her house, the twins were enjoying a cup of tea in the lounge.

"Where's Aunt Lucy?"

"Upstairs," Amber said between mouthfuls of cupcake. "She's just come back from a walk with Barry. Would you like a cup of tea?"

"Yes, please. I just need a quick word with Aunt Lucy, but I'll be back down in a minute. I'll have one of those cupcakes too."

Barry was so tired he could barely stand. Aunt Lucy was trying to dry him off with an enormous towel.

"Has it been raining over here?" I asked.

"Hi, Jill. No. Soft lad here decided he wanted to go for a swim in the lake."

"I only wanted to play with the ducks," Barry said.

"The ducks don't want to play with you. You scare them."

"I'm not scary, am I, Jill?"

"You are to a small duck. No more jumping in the lake. Promise?"

"I promise."

"There. That will have to do." Aunt Lucy got to her feet. Barry slumped to the floor, and closed his eyes.

"I wondered if you'd managed to find that 'schedule' spell?"

"Yes, I did. I put it in the cupboard in the kitchen. Let's go downstairs and have a cup of tea."

"This seems to be straightforward enough." I'd only glanced at the spell, but there was nothing in there that worried me unduly.

"You shouldn't have any problems with it. It might take you a while to set it up the first time, but once you've customised it to your needs, it should work like clockwork from then on."

"This is obviously the kind of spell that Agatha Crustie has been using. If she could handle it, I'm sure I'll be able to. Oh, by the way, did your friend find her pet?"

"Gloria? No. Not yet. She's really upset."

"Jill. Are you going to come with us tomorrow?" Pearl had come through from the lounge.

"We're going to collect the puppies." Amber was close behind her.

"Why not? I wouldn't mind another trip to Candle Sands. What did Alan and William say when you told them about the pups?"

"They weren't too keen at first, but they've come around to the idea," Amber said.

"Yeah, we know just how to get them to see things our way." Pearl grinned.

"I just bet you do."

I'd said my goodbyes, and just stepped out of the house when who should I bump into but an old friend of mine.

"Alicia."

"Jill."

"Aunt Lucy told me you'd moved in."

"Yeah. I'm with Glen now."

"There had better be no trouble."

"There won't be. I told your aunt that's all behind me now."

"You'll forgive me for being somewhat sceptical. You once told me that you were a solicitor, working in Washbridge, and then you proceeded to poison me."

"I know, and I'm ashamed of what I did. I realise it's no excuse, but Ma Chivers —"

"You can't blame everything on Ma Chivers. You knew what you were doing."

"Unless you've actually been under her influence, you can't possibly know what it's like. That doesn't excuse what I did, but now that I've found Glen, I just want to live a normal life like everyone else. I'll never go back to that life. I promise."

"Actions speak louder than words. Just remember what I said. One wrong step towards Aunt Lucy or any of my family, and you'll have me to answer to."

Chapter 9

As I was going to be working through the night in Chez Piper, I decided to go home and try to get a few hours' sleep first. Jack had sent me a message earlier, saying he would be late in. I'd replied and told him about my plans to do the nightshift. We were becoming more and more like ships in the night.

First, though, I needed something to eat, so I called in at the corner shop. A ready-meal would do just fine.

Little Jack Corner seemed a little taller.

"Hello, young lady."

"Hi, Jack. You seem taller today."

"How very observant of you. You're the first person to notice. I've replaced my box with an adjustable height platform." He pointed down at his feet.

I leaned over the counter to get a better view, and sure enough, he was standing on a small metal platform instead of the usual wooden box.

"Would you like to see how it works?"

"Sure." I would have preferred to get off home because I had a long night ahead of me, but I could see that he was keen to give a demonstration.

"Watch this." He took a gizmo from his pocket, pressed the small green button, and the platform gradually began to rise. "What do you think?"

"That's very impressive."

"And to lower it, I press the red button."

He did just that, but instead of going back down, the platform continued to rise, but much quicker now. Little Jack Corner was headed straight for the ceiling.

"Careful! You're going to hit your head!" I yelled at

him.

"It isn't working!" I could hear the panic in his voice.

"Grab my hand!"

He did, and I managed to pull him off the platform, and onto the counter top.

"Thank you. I could have been squashed."

"If I were you, I think I'd go back to the wooden box."

"It may just be teething problems. I'll give it another try later."

"If you do, make sure there's someone around to come to your rescue if it goes rogue again."

I passed him the ready-meal and a packet of custard creams.

"Anything else today? How about a bucket?"

"I'm okay for buckets, thanks."

"What about a nose spinner? They're all the rage." He pointed to the small display at the far end of the counter.

"I think you mean finger spinners, don't you?"

"No." He grabbed one, then lay back on the counter, and balanced the spinner on his nose. "Watch!" He set it spinning. "See!"

"Are you sure you're not supposed to spin it on your finger?"

"Why would you want to spin it on your finger?"

It was a fair question.

I was just about to leave when Little Jack called me back.

"You haven't heard the thought for the day."

"Sorry, I forgot."

"A stitch in time laughs longest."

"Great. Thanks for that."

As I left the shop, I ran into Missy Muffet, hand-in-hand

with a rather handsome young man.

"Hi, Missy. You'll need to keep an eye on Jack. That new platform of his seems to be on the blink."

"I'm not actually working today. I'm just here to collect my wages." She turned to the young man. "This is my boyfriend, Tommy. Tommy Tucker."

***

When Blake saw me pull onto my driveway, he came running across the road.

"Hi, Blake. I'm glad to see the trains have been removed."

"They had to bring in a tow-truck."

"It's about time those two men grew up, and stopped playing with their silly trains."

"You won't have to worry about Mr Kilbride for much longer."

"Why's that?"

"He told me earlier that he intends to sell up and move to Fleetwood."

"Oh? Why Fleetwood?"

"He has friends there. They're fishermen, apparently. He's tired of all the bickering with Hosey."

"I can't say I'll miss the bagpipes. I haven't seen much of you or Jen, recently. How are things?"

"Good, really good. I came over to tell you that Kilbride isn't the only one who will be moving out. We'll be moving away from Washbridge, too."

"How come?"

"We decided that we both needed a new start. My 'coming out' to Jen kind of upset things for a while, so we thought a reset was called for."

"What about your jobs?"

"We applied to run a pub. It's something we've both always fancied doing. We heard yesterday that we've been offered one in Northumberland. We have to go on a two-month course up there first, and then we take over the pub. It's called The Underworld. If you and Jack are ever in that neck of the woods, you must drop in."

"We will. When do you leave?"

"Next week."

"So soon?"

"The course starts the week after."

"I'll miss you. And Jen."

"Likewise. I really appreciate all the help you've given us."

He gave me a hug, and then made his way back across the road.

I would definitely miss Blake. He was the only other sup on the street, and someone with whom I could discuss things that I could never talk to Jack about.

**

As cardboard goes, the microwave meal wasn't too awful. The custard creams were, of course, as excellent as ever.

Before I grabbed some shut-eye, I wanted to set the 'schedule' spell so that the cleaning would get done the following day while both Jack and I were out at work. I'd already come up with spells which would control the vacuum, duster and other cleaning implements. All I needed now was to cast the spell which would schedule those individual tasks. Just as Aunt Lucy had suggested, the 'schedule' spell was actually very straightforward. Two o'clock in the afternoon seemed like a sensible time to set it for because Jack was never in at that time on a weekday. That would leave plenty of time for the spell to get all the work completed long before either of us got home. The more I thought about this new cleaning arrangement, the more I liked it. Not only would it save us money, but it would also mean that I got all the credit. I could then use that as leverage to persuade Jack that he should cook dinner every day.

What? Of course it's fair. A lot of effort goes into casting these spells. Snigger.

***

It was just as well that I'd set the alarm for ten o'clock because I was fast asleep when it sounded. I would have dearly loved to roll over, and sleep until morning, but I'd promised the Pipers that I'd keep watch at the restaurant overnight.

Jack was still not home when it was time for me to leave, so I left him a note on the kitchen table:

Didn't get chance to do the dishes. Sorry. xxx

What do you mean that wasn't very romantic? I gave him three kisses, didn't I? Sheesh.

It had just turned eleven when I arrived, bleary-eyed, at Chez Piper. The last few customers were being gently encouraged to vacate their tables and go home.

"Are you sure you'll be alright in here by yourself, Jill?" Mr Piper said.

"I'll be fine, but I'm going to need plenty of coffee to see me through the night."

"The coffee machine is over there in the corner. Just help yourself. Would you like anything to eat?"

"No, thanks. I had some cardboard earlier."

"Sorry?"

"I'm okay. You two can get off as soon as you're ready."

An hour later, I was on my own in the restaurant. There were two comfortable sofas in the reception area, but I daren't sit on those for fear that I might fall asleep. Instead, I took a seat at the table closest to the kitchen. All I had to do now was wait.

And wait.

By four o'clock in the morning, I was buzzing from the effects of the coffee, and yet my eyes still begged to close. I'd seen and heard nothing all night, and was beginning to think that it had been a waste of time, but then there was a noise. A soft pitter patter across the floor. I turned around, expecting to see someone, but there was no one there. The sound continued: pitter, patter—just like tiny footsteps. Then, the door to the kitchen swung open and closed as though someone had walked through it. I walked over to the kitchen door, and pushed it open as quietly as I could. When the gap was wide enough, I slipped inside.

The door to the storage room was ajar, and I could hear the sound of cupboards being opened and closed. Someone was in there. I tip-toed over to the door, and peered inside. There was no one to be seen, but I knew there was someone in there—whoever it was had obviously made themselves invisible. Was the thief a witch or a wizard? It seemed to be the only explanation.

I was still trying to decide how to play this when I

noticed that one of the open cupboards contained several large bags of flour, one of which was open. I grabbed it from the shelf, and launched it in the general direction of whoever was plundering the storeroom.

"Ouch! Stop it!" The squeaky little voice sounded quite pathetic. "Please don't hurt me!"

For a few moments, I was too stunned to speak. I'd expected the flour to reveal a witch or a wizard, but instead I found myself face to face with a small furry creature, which was standing on the worksurface.

"Who are you?" I yelled. "What are you doing in here?"

"I'm Furball. Please don't hurt me."

"I'm not going to hurt you. Where did you come from?"

"I don't know."

"You must know where you live."

"I live with Glow."

"Who's Glow?"

"The person I live with."

"Why aren't you with Glow now?"

"I got lost. You aren't going to put me in prison, are you?"

"Of course not. How exactly did you get lost?"

"I went outside for a walk, and it started to rain, so I climbed onto the back of a lorry. I think I must have fallen asleep because when I climbed out later, I didn't know where I was. I was lost. That's why I came in here."

"Did you jump out of the lorry while it was moving?"

"No. It had stopped. I got out and searched for Glow, but I couldn't find her so I came in here."

"I see. Do you mind if I ask what kind of creature you are?"

"I'm a Furball."

"I thought that was your name."

"That's right."

Huh? "You can't stay here."

"Can I go back to Glow?"

"When we find her, but for now, you'd better come with me."

"Are you a Glow, too?"

"No, I'm a Jill. Let's get everything tidied up in here first, and then we'll go."

I daren't take Furball to my office because I wasn't sure how he and Winky would get along. Even though Furball was invisible, Winky would probably pick up his scent. My only other option was to take him home with me until such time as I could find Glow — whoever she was.

I left a note for the Pipers, telling them that I had nothing to report, then I drove Furball home. It was five o'clock in the morning when I arrived back at the house. Jack's car was on the driveway.

When I opened the back door to lift Furball out, he was visible.

"I can see you," I said.

"I can see you, too."

"How come you aren't invisible? You have to make yourself invisible."

"I don't know how."

"But you were invisible earlier."

"That only happens when I get nervous."

"My partner, Jack, is a policeman. He's in the house right now, and if he sees you, he'll probably put you in prison."

"Yikes!" Furball disappeared in front of my eyes.

"That's better. Now come over here, and I'll carry you inside."

He nestled himself into my arms, and I made my way into the house. Once inside, I stopped at the bottom of the stairs to check if I could hear Jack. The house was silent.

"I'm going to put you in the spare bedroom," I whispered. "You'll have to stay in there until I come to get you later this morning. Okay?"

"Okay."

"And you must stay absolutely quiet."

"I will. I promise."

Chapter 10

"Jill. Wake up!" Jack nudged me.

"Go away. I didn't get home until five."

"It's eleven o'clock."

"Are you sure? It feels like I've only been asleep for five minutes." I grabbed my phone from the bedside cabinet. It really was eleven. "How come you haven't gone to work yet?"

"I didn't get much sleep either." He yawned.

"What time did you get in?"

"Just after midnight. Look, there's something we need to talk about."

"I need a drink first."

"Jill. This is important."

"What is?"

"I think the house is possessed."

I picked up the pillow and hit him around the head with it. "I thought you were being serious."

"I am. Deadly serious. At about two o'clock this morning, I heard noises downstairs. I thought it was you at first, but when I checked the window, I could see your car wasn't there. I figured it might be a burglar so I sneaked downstairs, and that's when I saw it."

"A ghost? Are you sure it wasn't just a shadow?"

"Not a ghost. The vacuum cleaner. It was vacuuming the lounge all by itself."

Oh bum!

"And a duster was wiping down the table."

"Did you by any chance have a few drinks when you got in last night?"

"No. None. When I grabbed hold of the vacuum, it

stopped, so I put it away. Same with the duster. Do you think we should get someone in to perform an exorcism?"

"No, I don't. Think about it. What's more likely? That the vacuum cleaner is possessed, or that you had a nightmare?"

"But it seemed so real."

"That kind of bad dream always does. I once dreamed I'd eaten a giant marshmallow, and when I woke up the pillow had disappeared."

"Okay, I get it. I'm being stupid." He laughed. "Whoever heard of a possessed duster?"

Phew! That had been a close call. I never was good with the twenty-four-hour clock. I must have set the 'schedule' spell for 2am instead of 2pm.

As soon as Jack had left for work, I went into the spare bedroom.

"Furball? Where are you?"

"Has the policeman gone?" His soft voice came from somewhere close by.

"Yes, he's gone to work."

"Are you sure? I don't want to go to prison."

"I'm positive."

"Phew!" Furball appeared, seated on an old ironing board.

"There you are. Did you sleep okay?"

"Yes, thanks. Can I go home to Glow now, please?"

"I have to find her first. Would you like something to eat?"

"Yes, please. I'm very hungry."

"What would you like?"

"Biscuits are my favourite food."

"Any particular kind?"

"Custard creams."

"I don't think I have any of those."

What? Okay, okay. I'd give up my last few custard creams. Happy now?

He really did like them. He scoffed the last five in the blink of an eye.

Plain greedy, if you ask me.

After I'd settled Furball back in the spare bedroom, I quickly adjusted the timing on the 'schedule' spell to avoid any further mishaps, and then I set off for work.

The outer office looked superb. The walls were now sky blue, and there were no streaks or splashes. Mrs V and Jules were both at their desks.

"What do you think of the office now?" I said.

"It looks great." Jules nodded her approval.

"I have to admit that I wasn't very confident when I saw who you'd brought in the second time," Mrs V said. "But he certainly knew his onions. It's just a pity about the low-flying nails."

"I guess I ought to take a look at my office."

"Before you do, Jill," Mrs V said. "Would it be okay to have some plants in here? They would finish the room off nicely."

"I'm not sure I can afford them."

"Don't worry about the cost. I have an old friend who owns a garden centre. He's always telling me that I'm welcome to help myself to a plant or two."

"A gentleman friend, eh?" I grinned. "Does Armi know about him?"

"There's nothing to know. Rodney Greenfinger is just a

good friend. So, would it be okay?"

"I don't see why not."

Nails had made an excellent job of my office too. That certificate of his had obviously been well deserved.

Winky was sitting on the sofa, looking very sorry for himself.

"What's up with you, Winky?"

He touched his throat with one paw, and mouthed some words, but I couldn't make out what he was trying to say.

"Sorry? What did you say?"

He jumped off the sofa, and walked across the room to me. "Sore throat," he whispered.

"Oh dear. I'm sorry to hear that." Tee-hee.

"It's a disaster. It's the choir competition tomorrow."

"It will probably be better by then."

"*Probably*? I can't rely on *probably*," he croaked. "Don't you realise what's at stake here? I need you to go and get me some syrup."

"I'm busy."

"Please! This is a matter of life and death. If I let down the rest of the choir, they'll disown me."

"What kind of syrup?"

"Feline throat syrup."

"Where would I find that?"

"At the pharmacy. Where do you think? The fishmonger?"

"I'd cut out the cheek if you want me to get it for you."

"Sorry. I'm just stressed out."

"I have to go out soon anyway. I'll bring some back with me."

"Thank you."

"Have you had any feedback from your gang about Leo Riley?"

"Nothing out of the ordinary to report so far." His voice was breaking up.

"Okay, tell them to keep on him. And then you should go and lie down to give your voice a rest."

***

So far, I only had the word of Christine Bold that her daughter had gone crazy. What if she'd somehow managed to get a perfectly sane woman locked up? It was very unlikely, but until I saw Jasmine for myself, I couldn't rule it out.

There was no way that Jasmine's mother would have given her blessing for me to pay her daughter a visit. But that wasn't a problem—I had my methods.

"I'm here to see my daughter." I was in the reception area of Washbridge Regent's Hospital.

"What's her name?"

"Jasmine Bold."

"Just a moment, please." The receptionist brought up the details on her computer screen.

A little research beforehand had revealed that their security system was based upon photographs. Next of kin, and any other authorised visitors, were required to have their photographs taken. These were checked at every visit.

The receptionist looked from her screen to me, and then back again. I wasn't concerned because I'd cast the 'doppelganger' spell, so when she looked at me, she was actually seeing Christine Bold.

"I have a note here to say that you're to see Dr Smythe, Mrs Bold."

"But I want to see my daughter. I want to see Jasmine."

"I'll just get hold of Dr Smythe." She picked up the phone. "He'll explain everything to you."

It was pointless arguing because she was already speaking to the doctor. After she'd hung up, she instructed me to take a seat.

Dr Smythe, a ruddy-faced man in his sixties, appeared a few minutes later.

"Sorry to keep you waiting, Mrs Bold."

"I want to see my daughter."

"Please come to my office." He led the way down a long corridor. I had no option but to follow.

"What's this all about?" I demanded, once we were in his office. "Is Jasmine alright?"

"She's taken a turn for the worse, I'm afraid."

"She isn't dead, is she?"

"No, nothing like that. Her behaviour has become much more manic. She's far too dangerous for you to see her."

"Can't you sedate her?"

"We have. We've given her as much as we dare."

"I want to see her."

"Just a second." He sat at his desk, and brought up a split-screen display that appeared to be some sort of CCTV output. When he clicked on one of the small squares, it expanded to fill the screen.

What I saw horrified me. A young woman, wearing a white robe, was pacing back and forth in what appeared to be a padded room. There was no sound, but it was obvious that she was screaming. Every now and then, she would throw herself onto the ground, and begin to flail her arms and legs around.

"She can't hurt herself in there," the doctor said, but his words were hardly reassuring. "You can see now why it isn't safe for you to go inside."

I most definitely could.

"Do you have any similar cases?"

"I'm afraid I'm not at liberty to discuss that."

In that case, my dear doctor, it's time for your nap.

I cast the 'sleep' spell, and quickly used the mouse to go back to the main screen. From there, I checked the images from the other cells. I soon found two other young women who were acting just like Jasmine Bold.

While the doctor was still asleep, I checked Jasmine's screen again. She was still acting like she was possessed. This time, though, I noticed a small 'I' symbol in the top righthand corner of the screen. When I clicked on it, it brought up her details: name, age and address. I quickly located the same information for the other two women, and made a note of it in my phone. After reversing the 'sleep' spell, I cast the 'forget' spell on the doctor, and then made my exit.

What I'd seen had been truly shocking, but it also eliminated the possibility that this was the work of either her boyfriend or her mother. Whatever had affected her so badly, had also affected the other two women. I had to find out what connected them, and what had caused them to fall into that dreadful state.

***

What I'd seen at the hospital had been very upsetting. If Christine Bold had seen her daughter in that state, she would have been traumatised.

I needed something to take my mind off those horrors, and I knew just the thing to do it. Blueberries, especially when covered in muffin, are a little known natural remedy.

What? Of course it's true.

Now that the threat of the giant triangle had been lifted, it was safe to return to Coffee Triangle. Or at least, it would have been if I'd been able to get down the high street. Blocking my way was a huge crowd; they were watching the parade, which was marching up and down the road. There was all manner of circus acts, including: clowns (yuk!), jugglers and stilt-walkers. Leading the parade was a marching band, dressed in matching uniforms, which were a similar colour to my outer office. Several huge banners were being held aloft, all of which read:

The Grand Re-Opening of EVER – The Destination!

It took a while, but I eventually managed to fight my way through the crowd to Grandma's shop, which was no longer boarded up. The first thing I noticed was the new sign which now read simply: **EVER**

When I eventually managed to get inside, I barely recognised the place. All of the yarn had gone. So too had the old sales counter. What had once been the shop floor was now part of the extended tea room; it was heaving with customers.

"Jill!" Kathy called to me.

"What are you wearing?" I laughed.

"Shut up or I shall be forced to kill you."

"What's going on in here?"

"Your grandmother has closed down the yarn sales, and turned this place into a — err — "

"Destination?"

"Yeah, that's what she insists we call it. As you can see, the whole of the ground floor is now the tea room. The roof terrace is still there, and so is the new ballroom."

"And what are you supposed to be?"

I couldn't tear my eyes away from the red trouser suit.

"We're the Everettes."

"You're what?" I almost choked.

"That's what she insists on calling us: Everettes. Have you ever heard of anything so stupid?"

"I take it Chloe and Maria are *Everettes* too?"

"Oh yes. I feel sorry for Maria. She's only just started here, and doesn't know what's hit her. If it stays as busy as this, we're going to need a lot more staff."

"Miss!" someone called. "Hey, Everette!"

"I think you've been summoned."

It was way too crowded for my liking, so I started back towards the door.

"What do you think of the place?" Grandma appeared from nowhere.

"You've got rid of the yarn."

"As always, your powers of observation astound me."

"Why have you done that? Just because Ma Chivers has opened up a shop across the road?"

"Of course not. I could easily have seen her off. I was growing tired of the yarn business. It was time for a change. This is far more exciting, don't you think?"

"I suppose so. What about all the people who have

bought Everlasting Wool subscriptions?"

"They'll be okay, as long as they keep paying their money. If we get any new enquiries, we'll refer them across the road. Ma is welcome to them. Just look how busy it is in here."

"It certainly seems to be a hit."

"I'm going to need more staff. Are you sure I can't tempt you to become an Everette?"

"Bye, Grandma."

Chapter 11

I'd promised to meet the twins at Aunt Lucy's house. We were going back to Candle Sands to collect their puppies. While I was there, I hoped to take a look around the lighthouse.

"Mum can't come with us," Pearl said in a hushed voice.

The twins and I were in the hallway; Aunt Lucy was talking to someone in the lounge.

"Why not?" I whispered. "Who's in there with her?"

"It's her friend, Gloria."

"The one who's lost her pet?"

"Yeah." Amber nodded. "He's still missing. Mum's trying to comfort her."

Just then, Aunt Lucy came out of the lounge, and closed the door behind her.

"Have the girls told you I can't come?"

"We could wait until your friend has left," I offered.

"I've promised to stay here and help her with the search. To be honest, after all this time, I don't hold out much hope, but I daren't say that to Gloria. She's upset enough as it is. Take the keys to Lester's car, Jill. You can drive."

"Why can't I drive it?" Pearl pouted.

"Or me?" Amber said.

"Because I've seen you two behind the wheel. Jill is a much better driver." Aunt Lucy fished the keys out of her coat pocket, and handed them to me.

"*Jill is a much better driver,*" Pearl mocked from the back seat, as we were about to set off.

"*Oh, yes. Much better.*" Amber joined in.

"There's no point in your having a go at me. I'd have been quite happy for either one of you to drive."

"Move over then." Amber grabbed the steering wheel.

"I can't. Not now that Aunt Lucy has entrusted the driving to me. Do you two want to get your puppies or not?"

"I don't see why we couldn't have taken the train like last time," Pearl said.

"Because trying to bring back two puppies on the train would be a nightmare. You have put the cage in the back, haven't you?"

"Yes, it's in there." Amber was growing impatient. "Now, are we going, or aren't we?"

The roads in Candlefield were a joy to drive on—so much quieter than those in the human world. And, much to my relief, the car seemed to know its way to the seaside resort. The only thing that slightly marred the journey was the twins' constant questioning: *Are we nearly there yet? How much longer?*

"We're here now!" I pulled into the car park on the cliff top.

"Come on, Jill. I want to see my puppy." Amber was out of the car almost before it had come to a halt. "He's so cute!"

"My puppy is cuter than yours." Pearl scrambled out of the back door.

"I'm going to take a look around the lighthouse. Why don't you two go and collect your puppies, and meet me back here in an hour? You've got the address, I assume."

"Of course we have." Amber rolled her eyes. "We're not stupid."

"Girls! Wait!" I called after them.

"What now, Jill?" Pearl sighed.

"The cage?"

"Oh yeah." Amber opened the boot, grabbed the cage, and then the two of them raced off.

As I walked along the cliff top towards the lighthouse, I noticed that the large light was actually on. That struck me as strange because it was broad daylight, and Duncan O'Nuts had told me of his struggle to pay the candle bill. Why then waste candles by burning them during the daytime?

A small white-stone cottage, which I took to be the keeper's accommodation, was built onto the base of the lighthouse. The solid wooden door barely registered my knock, but then I noticed a black metal chain—I gave it a pull, and heard the clap of a bell inside the house.

"Hello, deary." The woman who answered the door was wearing a white apron over a paisley-patterned smock dress. "Can I help you?"

"Mrs O'Nuts?"

"That's right, deary."

"Is Duncan in?"

"He's up top at the moment." She gestured to the top of the lighthouse. "Would you like to come in and wait for him?"

"Yes, please."

The small cottage was beautiful, but it did have a strange odour which I couldn't quite place. Incense probably, although I couldn't see any.

"Tea, coffee, orange juice?" She led the way into a tiny kitchen fitted out with oak cupboards and furniture.

"Tea would be lovely. I'm Jill, by the way."

"Nice to meet you, Jill. I'm Maude. How do you like your tea?"

"Milk and two-thirds spoonfuls of sugar, please."

"Two-thirds?"

"I know it's a little precise, but—"

"Not at all. My friend, Rosemary Teacup, always insists on four-fifths. That can be a little tricky."

A few minutes later, I heard footsteps above us.

"Duncan's on his way." Maude held out a tin of biscuits. Another mixed-biscuit travesty.

"No, thanks."

"Duncan. We have a visitor."

"Oh?"

I stood up. "We met a couple of days ago. You were collecting for the lighthouse."

"Right, yes, of course. I remember."

"Did you realise that the main light is still on?"

"Is it? I must have forgotten to shut it down. Did you want something in particular?"

"I was hoping to take a look around the lighthouse. When I saw you before, you said—"

"Sorry. I—err—have an urgent appointment."

"You never mentioned anything," Maude said.

"I forgot."

"What about the light?" I said. "Shouldn't you shut it down before you go?"

"No time. I'm running late." He grabbed his coat, and moments later, was out of the door.

"I do apologise for my husband." Maude tutted. "He isn't normally so rude, but he's been under a lot of pressure lately."

"Finding the funds to keep this place going can't be easy. He must be under a lot of stress."

"He is. That's why I insisted we take a trip to Candlefield yesterday. We had a lovely day. We did a little shopping, spent some time in the park, and visited the elf museum, and the pixie king's palace gardens—they're so beautiful. I'd hoped the day out would take his mind off things, and I thought it had. When he came back, he seemed much brighter, but—well—it doesn't seem to have lasted."

"How is your dog? It's Bonny, isn't it?"

"She's doing well. We're expecting the pups any moment now. I can't let you see her, I'm afraid."

"I understand."

"I apologise again for Duncan. Normally, he loves to show people around."

"No problem. He's obviously very busy. I'll try again the next time I'm down here." I finished the last of my drink. "That was a lovely cup of tea, thanks. You won't forget to remind him about the light, will you?"

"I won't. It was nice to meet you, Jill."

I could see the twins weren't back yet, so I had a quick walk onto the beach below, making sure to keep my eyes peeled for sand demons. The only people on there were dogwalkers. Everyone else must have been put off by the strong wind, and the drizzle which had just started to fall.

"Jill! We're back!" Pearl yelled from the cliff-top above. The two of them were carrying the cage between them.

"I'll be with you in a minute."

"Well, aren't you two just adorable?" I poked my finger through the cage, and the puppies fell over one another, trying to lick it.

"Mine is the most handsome, don't you think, Jill?" Amber said.

"Rubbish. Tommy is much better looking," Pearl scoffed.

"Is that what you're going to call him? Tommy?"

Pearl nodded. "He looks like a Tommy, don't you think?"

"Mine is called Timmy," Amber said.

"You'd better put Tommy and Timmy's cage on the back seat."

"I want to sit in the back with them," Amber said.

"No, I want to go in the back," Pearl objected.

"If you put the cage in the middle, you'll both be able to squeeze in there." And that way, I might actually get some peace and quiet.

"Did you get to see the lighthouse?" Pearl asked, once we were back on the road.

"No. The lighthouse keeper was too busy to show me around. I did get a cup of tea though."

I dropped the twins and their new puppies back at their respective houses, and then I took the car back to Aunt Lucy's.

"Aunt Lucy! I'm back!" I called from the hallway. I didn't want to burst in on her in case she was still with her friend.

"Success?" Aunt Lucy came through from the lounge. "Did you get the puppies?"

"We did. I dropped the twins back home. Has your

friend gone?"

"Gloria? Yes. We've only just finished searching. No luck, I'm afraid."

"It makes you wonder if having a dog is worth it with all that worry."

"A dog? It isn't a dog. It's a loop bear. Have you ever seen one?"

"I've never even heard of them."

"They're quite small. Just a little ball of fur. In fact, that's what Gloria calls hers: Furball."

"Hold on. These loop bears? They don't by any chance turn invisible when they're scared or nervous, do they?"

"Yes. That's why it took Gloria a while to realise that Furball was actually missing."

"Your friend? Does everyone call her Gloria?"

"No, only me. I've known her since school, and she'll always be Gloria to me. Almost everyone else calls her Glo."

"In that case, I may have some good news for Gloria."

***

After I'd told Aunt Lucy that I had Furball in my house, she'd got straight on the phone to her friend. The three of us had magicked ourselves over to Smallwash, where the grand reunion had taken place. Furball had been so excited to see his 'Glow' that he'd practically licked her face off.

The cute little bear had obviously fallen asleep in the back of a lorry bound for the human world. When he'd woken, he was just on the outskirts of Washbridge. Scared and invisible, he must have taken refuge in the first building he came to, which just happened to be Chez Piper.

I made a call.

"Mrs Piper? It's Jill."

"Hi, Jill."

"No more missing food, I assume?"

"No, but we did find traces of flour on the kitchen floor."

"That was down to me. Sorry about that. Look, I really think that whoever was doing this must have got the message that you're onto them. I highly doubt they'll do it again."

"I'd still like to know who it was."

"I know, but I doubt that's going to happen now. Why don't you give it a while — maybe a week? If anything else is stolen, give me a call, and I'll be straight over, but I have a hunch you won't have any more problems."

"I hope you're right. We'll see how it goes, then."

I wasn't really all that keen on pets — apart from Barry, and Winky obviously. But then, I didn't really consider Winky a pet — more a pain in the backside. Still, I could certainly have gone for a loop bear — they were just so adorable. That was never going to happen though. How would I explain to Jack that our tiny bear-like pet could make itself invisible?

Oh bum!

I'd totally forgotten about Winky's throat syrup. If I didn't get it, I'd never hear the end of it. Then again, if I didn't get it, he probably wouldn't be able to talk to me.

So very tempting.

"Can I help you, Madam?" The bespectacled pharmacist, dressed in a white coat, approached me. I'd been studying the labels on the throat syrup bottles for the last ten minutes. Who knew there were so many?

"I'm looking for a particular kind of throat syrup."

"Which one?"

"Feline."

"That's not a brand I've heard of."

"Feline isn't the brand name. I mean feline as in: for cats. Do you stock it?"

"Of course we don't. This is a pharmacy—not a vets." He was still tutting to himself when he walked away.

"Pssst! Hey, over here!"

The young woman behind the cash desk, was beckoning to me. As I approached her, I realised she was a witch. She bent down, opened the cupboard below her till, and produced a small bottle.

"This is what you're after."

Sure enough, the label read: Feline Throat Syrup.

"Thanks. You're a life-saver. How much is it?"

"Ten-pounds and fifty-pence, please."

"It's how much?"

Chapter 12

When I got back to the office, Mrs V had a face like thunder.

"Whatever is wrong?"

"I will swing for your grandmother."

I should have known. "What has she done this time?"

"Look!" Mrs V held up a handful of broken knitting needles.

"Aren't those the free ones you got from Yarnstormers? What happened to them?"

"Your grandmother came charging in here, snatched them from my hand, and snapped them into pieces."

"Why?"

"How would I know? She didn't say a word. She's done the same with Jules' needles too." Mrs V pointed to the broken needles lying on the adjacent desk. "I understand she might be upset because she has competition now, but there's no excuse for this."

"You're right. It's unforgiveable, but I can't believe this can have anything to do with her being scared of the competition. She's just closed down her yarn operations."

"That's the first I've heard of it."

"You obviously haven't been down the high street today. Ever A Wool Moment is no more. It's now Ever, the destination."

"What's that when it's at home?"

"A tea room, roof terrace and ballroom. And, of course, the Everettes."

"The what?"

"Never mind. I have a couple of things to do, but then I'll go and see Grandma to find out what she's up to."

"You can tell her we want compensation for these needles."

Winky began to remonstrate silently with me. From his gestures and facial expressions, I gathered he wasn't best pleased at having to wait so long for his throat syrup.

"Here you are."

He snatched it from my hand, unscrewed the top, and took a swig.

"Steady on. I don't think you're supposed to drink it like that."

He shrugged and took another drink, then he managed to croak, "It took you long enough, didn't it? I asked you to buy it, not manufacture it."

"I'm sorry it took a while, but I've been busy. Do you know how much that cost?"

"You can't put a price on one's voice."

"Just as long as 'one' realises he owes me twelve pounds."

What? The mark-up was to cover my time, and the wear and tear on my shoes.

***

"Do, Re, Mi, Fa, Sol, La, Ti, Do. Do, Re, Mi, Fa, Sol, La, Ti, Do."

Oh no!

"I'm not sure you should be straining your voice yet. You only took the syrup half an hour ago."

"I feel fine. That stuff works wonders."

"Even so. Maybe you should wait a while before you do any more singing. Say, when I've gone home?"

"Jill," Mrs V appeared in the doorway. "There's a Mr Dewey to see you."

"Really? Okay, send him through, would you?"

"Is that cat of yours alright?" Mrs V glared at Winky.

"Yeah, why?"

"There was the most awful din coming from in here just now."

"It must have been coming from outside. I haven't heard anything."

"Cheek!" Winky said, after she'd gone to collect Stewey. "What does she know about singing, anyway?"

"Just keep quiet while my visitor is here."

The transformation in the man was amazing. The last time I'd seen Stewey Dewey, he'd looked like a homeless man, and he'd been so depressed that I'd genuinely feared he might do something stupid. Today, he looked as though he'd stepped out of the pages of a men's fashion magazine. He'd had a haircut, his face was clean-shaven, and his clothes were immaculate.

"I wouldn't have recognised you," I admitted.

"And it's all thanks to you, Jill. If you hadn't persuaded me to welcome Harry and Larry into my life, well—I—err— don't even want to think about it."

"I'm so pleased for you. It was terrible to see you blaming yourself for something that wasn't your fault. Have you seen much of Harry and Larry?"

"I can't get rid of them." He laughed. "Not that I'm complaining. They've given me a new lease of life. We're busy planning the new bakery. I tell you, Jill, I haven't felt so excited about anything for years."

"That's great. You must let me know when it opens."

"You'll be the guest of honour on opening day."

"Does that mean I get a muffin?"

"You get free muffins for life."

Now you're talking!

***

When I arrived at Ever, Kathy and the other Everettes were busy taking orders and serving drinks. Grandma's office was still in the same place, although the door had been repainted in a pleasing shade of red, to fit in with the new décor.

"Can you hear that?" Grandma said. She had her feet in a foot spa.

"Hear what?"

"The sound of tills ringing up the takings."

"Kathy and the others look run off their feet."

"That's what I pay them for, isn't it? I hope you aren't here to stir up industrial unrest among my staff again."

"I'm not. I'm here to find out why you broke Mrs V's and Jules' knitting needles?"

"That's the wrong question."

"Sorry?"

"You should be sorry. The correct question is why didn't *you* break them?"

"I have no idea what you're talking about."

"You're supposed to be the most powerful witch in Candlefield." She scoffed. "And yet, you didn't realise that Ma Chivers had cast a spell on all the knitting needles she gave away."

"Are you sure?"

"Of course I'm sure. You don't think she'd give

away for free without some ulterior motive, do you?"

"Which is?"

"I haven't worked that out yet, but whatever it is, you can guarantee it won't be good."

"Is there anything I can do?"

"Just try to placate Annabel and her sidekick, would you? I don't need any aggravation from them while I'm trying to get to the bottom of what Ma Chivers is up to."

"Okay, and I'm sorry for not trusting you."

***

As I drove home, I thought about what Grandma had said. She was right; I should have realised the knitting needles had been compromised. What exactly was Ma Chivers up to? Hopefully, Grandma would get to the bottom of it before it was too late.

Mr Ivers was in the toll booth, but he wasn't the one collecting the toll fees. Instead, a young man, who looked no more than sixteen, was taking the payments while Mr Ivers was watching something on his tablet.

"Hello, Mr Ivers."

"Hello, Jill. I was just catching up on Toppers Tales. Do you watch it?"

"It's not really my thing. I see you have a little helper."

"This is my nephew, Bert. Say hello to Jill, Bert."

"Hello," Bert said.

"I'm paying Bert to collect the toll fees for me. The constant back and forth plays havoc with my elbows."

"Isn't that the sum total of your job? Collecting the toll fees?"

"And, I'm doing just that. Bert is just acting as my

surrogate."

"If you're making so much money from the Toppers newsletter, wouldn't it be simpler just to give up this job?"

"Yes, but there's the pension to consider. The newsletter pays well now, but there's no pension provision. Paying Bert to take the cash allows me to get the best of both worlds. Plus, it earns a little pocket money for Bert, doesn't it, Bert?"

"Yes."

A man of few words was Bert.

Megan was washing her van when I arrived home.

"Hi, Megan. You can clean my car afterwards, if you like."

"No, thanks." She smiled. "I hate cleaning the van, but I have to maintain the right image for the business. While you're here, could I have a quick word inside?" She gestured to her house.

"Sure. I mustn't be too long though. It's my turn to cook dinner."

"It will only take a minute."

Once inside, I could tell Megan was struggling to say whatever it was that was on her mind.

"Is something wrong, Megan?"

"Not wrong exactly. I'm just worried you'll think I've lost my marbles if I ask you this."

"I hear and see some pretty weird things in my job. I doubt you'll shock me."

"Okay, but you must promise not to repeat this to anyone. Not even Jack."

"I promise."

"I think something is wrong with me."

"Are you ill?"

"Not ill exactly. I just keep getting these weird urges."

"What kind of urges?" Did I really want to know?

"I'm afraid this is going to sound gross."

"Come on, Megan, you may as well tell me now."

"I keep wondering what it would be like to—err—well, to bite someone's neck, and drink their blood." She covered her face with her hands. "You must think I'm a complete whack job."

"Not at all. We all have crazy thoughts sometimes. I occasionally think I'm a witch with magical powers."

"Do you really, Jill?" She looked up. "You're not just saying that to make me feel better?"

"No, it's true. I think most people have thoughts like that—they just don't admit to them."

"You don't think I'm turning into a vampire, then?"

"No more than I am a witch."

"Phew! What a relief. I'm so glad I spoke to you."

"Okay, well, I'd better get going."

"Thanks again, Jill."

"No problem."

Oh bum! I felt another visit to WashBets coming on.

While I'd been in Megan's house, Jack had arrived home.

"Are you sure you don't want us to find another cleaner, Jill?" He had the dustpan and brush in his hands.

"No. I'm going to do it myself."

"There's what looks like animal fur all over the kitchen floor. You didn't bring that mangy old cat of yours here today, did you?"

"Of course I didn't, and Winky isn't mangy."

"Where did all this fur come from, then?"

I shrugged.

When Gloria had come over to collect Furball, she'd brought some of his favourite biscuits with her. He must have shed the fur while he was eating them in the kitchen.

It was time to change the subject.

"Some of our neighbours are leaving," I said.

"Who?"

"Mr Kilbride. He's fed up of the train-wars with Mr Hosey."

"It's a pity we can't get rid of both of them."

"And Blake and Jen."

"Really? I'll be sorry to see them go. Why are they leaving?"

"They're going to manage a pub in Northumberland."

"Sometimes, I think we should throw all of this in, and make a new start somewhere else."

"Doing what?"

"We could open a bowling shop. That would be great, wouldn't it?"

"Let me think. No, it would be terrible. Talking of shops. Grandma has changed the name of her shop to just Ever, and has closed down all the yarn sales. It is now a *destination*."

"What's that exactly?"

"It's basically the old shop minus the wool, but with lots more red trouser suits."

"Sorry?"

"Not as sorry as Kathy is. She's no longer a shop assistant or a manager. She is now officially an Everette."

"A what?"

"An Everette, and she has to wear a horrible, red trouser

suit."

"You shouldn't laugh, Jill."

"I know." I grabbed my phone.

"Who are you calling?"

"Shush." I waited for Kathy to pick up. "Kathy, it's me. Are you back home?"

"Yes, thank goodness. My feet are killing me."

"I'm really sorry to hear that. It isn't fair what Grandma has done."

"Maria and Chloe are fed up too. Why did you call?"

"Are you still wearing your uniform?"

"I haven't had time to change yet. I was just about to do it when you called."

"Would you do me a favour?"

"What?"

"Could you get Peter or one of the kids, to take a photo of you in your Everette trouser suit? I want to show it to Jack. Kathy? Kathy?" She'd hung up.

What a spoilsport!

Chapter 13

The next morning when I arrived at work, I had to struggle to get through the door because something was blocking it. When I eventually managed to force it open, and squeeze inside, I realised what the problem was. The outer office was full of tall potted plants—hundreds of them. I couldn't see anything for the foliage. There did however seem to be a narrow winding path through the jungle, so I followed it until I arrived at Jules' desk.

"Morning, Jill."

"What's going on? Where did all of these plants come from?"

"Annabel's friend, Mr Greenfinger, brought them in."

"Is he insane?"

"Shush!" She put her finger to her lips. "He's still here."

"Where?"

She pointed towards where the door to my office would normally be. "Good luck."

It wasn't luck, but a machete that I needed. "Hello? Mr Greenfinger?"

"Over here. Follow my voice."

"Please keep talking so I can find you."

"Okay. Once upon a time, there were three bears—"

"Ah, there you are, Mr Greenfinger."

"Call me Rod. Everyone does. I assume you must be Jill. Annabel has told me a lot about you." He laughed. "Don't worry—I didn't believe half of it."

Huh?

"Mrs V said that you were going to let her have some plants for the office, but I didn't realise there would be quite so many. There are an awful lot of them in here."

"Do you think she'll be pleased? I've been sweet on Annabel for as long as I can remember. This is my big chance to make a good impression on her."

"Did you know she was seeing someone at the moment?"

"Yes." He frowned. "That's why I have to work extra hard to win her over. Do you think this will do the trick?"

"Maybe."

The poor man sounded so desperate that I didn't have the heart to tell him to take his stupid plants away. I'd just have to put up with the jungle—at least until Mrs V had had the chance to see it in all its glory.

"Jill Gooder, I presume." Winky greeted me; he was wearing a safari suit and hat.

"What have you come as?" I laughed.

"That jungle next door is expanding fast. I thought I'd better be prepared."

"Good plan."

"Seriously, though, what's going on? This is nuts even by your standards."

"Don't blame me. All I did was agree that Mrs V could have a few plants in the office. I hadn't expected Jungle Rodney to try to turn this place into the Amazonian jungle. How is your throat? It sounds much better."

"Good as new, and just in time for the competition tonight."

"I take it you're feeling confident?"

"It's a foregone conclusion. The other choirs might as well stay at home."

***

I had the name and contact details of two of the other women who were in Washbridge Regent's Hospital with symptoms identical to those of Jasmine Bold.

Andrea Teller's next of kin was listed as her mother, Sarah Teller. When I'd called her, she'd readily agreed to see me. She lived not too far from Kathy's house.

"Jill? Do come in. My husband wanted to be here, but he has an urgent meeting at work. Can I get you anything to drink?"

"No, thanks. I'm okay."

She led the way into the dining room where there were numerous framed photographs on the walls and on the bookcase.

"Are these all Andrea?"

"Yes. She's an only child. Please, have a seat. Do you know what might have caused this terrible illness?"

"Not at the moment. Sorry."

"You mentioned that there were others who have been struck down with the same thing. Why hasn't anyone told me that?"

"I can't speak for the hospital, but it's possible that they don't want to cause mass panic. As I said on the phone, I've seen CCTV footage of Andrea and a number of other patients. Based on what I saw, the symptoms looked identical, but I could be wrong. I'm not a medical professional. The reason I wanted to speak to you is to find out how your daughter fell ill. That should give me a feel for if there's any connection."

"There really isn't that much to tell. One day she was perfectly well, and the next, it was as though she was possessed. I've never been so terrified in my life. I thought she was going to kill herself. Or me."

"And there were no other symptoms before that? She hadn't been complaining of feeling ill?"

"Nothing. I wish there was more I could tell you."

"That's okay. In fact, what you've described matches the story told by the mother of another patient being held in Regent's Hospital. She said her daughter had shown no prior signs, and that the illness had struck totally out of the blue. Tell me, is Andrea seeing anyone at the moment?"

"No." Sarah hesitated. "At least, I don't think so. She doesn't like to talk about her boyfriends with me. She says I'm too critical. I don't mean to be; I'm just trying to look out for her—that's all."

"Where does Andrea work?"

"She's a hairdresser in a salon called Total Cuts; they're in the city centre."

"Had she had any time off work prior to this happening?"

"No. Andrea loves her job. This is the first time she's had any time off ill since she started there."

We talked for a little while longer, and then Sarah provided me with a list of Andrea's closest friends. Before I contacted them, I wanted to check in on her place of work. The chances were that Andrea's fellow employees would see more of her on a day-to-day basis than her mother did. Maybe one of them had noticed a change in her prior to the onset of the illness.

***

The young man behind reception in Total Cuts took one

look at my hair, frowned, and said, "Oh dear."

Charming!

And then before I could tell him why I was there, he began with his critique, "Who has been doing your hair? Whoever it is should be shot. Still, you're in good hands now. Who is your appointment with?"

"I don't actually have an appointment."

"Not to worry. Seeing as it's an emergency, I'm sure we'll be able to slot you in, but you may have a short wait. Would you like a drink?"

"No, thanks. I'm not actually here to get my hair done."

"You're not? Are you sure?"

"I was hoping to speak to someone about Andrea Teller."

"Andy? How is she? We've all been frantic about her."

"Still very poorly, I'm afraid. Who would be the best person to talk to? Who knew Andy best?"

"Me probably. We're besties."

"Is there somewhere we could speak in private?"

"Sure." He turned towards the main salon. "Ginger! Come and take over the desk, would you? I have to speak to this lady about Andy."

Ginger, whose blonde hair revealed tell-tale ginger roots, came over. "How is Andy?"

"She's still very poorly, I'm afraid."

Once we were in the back office, the young man introduced himself as Carl.

"Andy and I started here at more or less the same time. She loves her job. I think she'd come here even if they didn't pay her. Not me. I'm only here for the money."

"Had you noticed anything different about Andy before she went off ill? Had she mentioned feeling poorly?"

"Nothing. She's never ill. And even when she was a bit under the weather, she'd still turn up for work. I told her she was silly. You wouldn't catch me coming to work with the flu. I'd be wrapped up in bed with a Beechams Powder and a good book."

"Was she at work the day before she fell ill?"

"Yes. We were talking about our holiday plans."

"Was she in a relationship, as far as you know?"

"Yes." He pulled a face. "Unfortunately."

"Why do you say that?"

"Andy is a darling, but she really knows how to pick 'em. I tried to warn her off this latest one, but did she listen to Carl? Of course she didn't."

"What's his name?"

"I don't know. Brutus, probably. He looks like a thug—tattoos and piercings everywhere. Don't get me wrong, I have nothing against tattoos or piercings, but there are limits. And that shaved head of his? Please!"

Tattoos, piercings and a shaved head? He had to be describing Billy Bhoy.

"How long had Andy been seeing this guy?"

"I'm not sure. Not long. He popped into the shop to pick her up after work a couple of times. He gives me the creeps."

"Thanks. You've been very helpful. I'll leave you my card just in case you think of anything else that might help."

"Are you sure you wouldn't like me to do something with your hair while you're here?"

Cheek!

***

When I got back to the office, someone had at least moved the plants away from the door, so I was able to get inside.

"Hello?" Mrs V's voice came from somewhere in the jungle. "Can I help you?"

"It's me, Mrs V."

"Jill. Sorry, I couldn't see you."

"How can I get to you?"

"Take the path on the right."

There were now two paths in front of me, so I did as instructed, and took the one on the right.

"I'm really sorry about all of this." Mrs V looked a little sheepish. "When I asked Rodney if he could let me have a few plants for the office, I never expected anything like this."

"He's trying to impress you. You do realise that he's sweet on you, don't you?"

"I suspected as much, but even so, this is rather extreme."

"You're going to have to tell him to get rid of them."

"That would be throwing kindness in his face."

"We can't function like this. What will the clients think when they see it?"

"What clients?"

"Mrs V!"

"Sorry, dear. You're right, of course. I just don't want to upset Rodney."

"You'll have to, I'm afraid."

"Okay. I'll give him a call."

Just then, my phone rang.

"Is that Jill?"

"Speaking."

"It's Karen Coombes. We met the other day in Spooky Wooky."

"Oh, yes. Hi, Karen."

"I said I'd give you a call when I'd managed to gather a few people together who have been affected by Hauntings Unlimited. I did try to call you yesterday, but I couldn't get through for some reason. There are quite a few of us gathered in GT Community Hall. I don't suppose there's any chance you could pop over now, is there? It should only take a few minutes."

"Yes, okay. I'll be there shortly."

"I have to nip out again, Mrs V. Please try to get this lot sorted before I get back, would you?"

"I will, dear."

"Jill!" Jules' voice came from somewhere to my left.

"Oh? Hi, Jules. I hadn't realised you were still here."

"Did you find out why your grandmother broke our knitting needles?"

"Not yet," I lied. "I'll let you know if I do."

I was starving, so on my way to the GT community hall, I popped into Spooky Wooky to pick up a muffin.

"Anything to drink, Jill?" Larry said.

"No, thanks. Just the muffin."

"Shall I put it in a bag?"

"No need. I'm going to eat it now. Incidentally, Stewey Dewey called in to see me. He's looking so much better."

"He is, isn't he? The plans for the new bakery are coming on a treat."

"Stewey said I'll get free muffins for life."

"Did he now?" Larry grinned. "There go our profits then."

"Got to rush. Catch you later."

When Karen Coombes had told me that there were a few people gathered in the community hall, she'd rather undersold it. The place was packed. It took a while for me to fight my way to the front.

"Excuse me. Non-dead coming through. Excuse me, please. Thank you."

"Jill, you made it," Karen greeted me.

"I didn't realise there would be so many people here."

"This scam has been going on for a long time. Shall we go onto the stage?"

I followed her onto the small stage where there were just two seats.

"Quiet please!" Karen had to yell to be heard. "Jill Gooder has joined us now."

"Hi, everyone."

After the crowd had eventually fallen silent, Karen continued, "It would probably be best if I give you a quick rundown on what has been happening, Jill."

"That would be great."

And she did. The gist of it was that ghosts in GT were being recruited by an outfit called Hauntings Unlimited. The company provided ghosts to establishments in the human world who wanted to market themselves as 'haunted houses'. The majority of their customers were stately homes and the like. As she was talking, it struck me that Washbridge House should have availed themselves of a service such as this one.

"The company simply isn't paying us the money that it owes us." Karen said. "Typically, they'll pay for the first month, but then the payments stop." She turned to the audience. "Isn't that right?"

There was lots of nodding and shouting in agreement.

"I was working in a country house in North Wales." A tall man near the front stepped forward. "I was quite lucky because I actually got paid for three months, but since then I've had nothing. Just lots of empty promises."

"Same here!" a woman shouted. "I was in Dorset. I've been chasing them for weeks, but getting nowhere."

The next few minutes were filled with stories that all followed the same pattern.

"Who runs the company?" I asked.

"This end of the operation is run by a guy called Kelvin Toastmaster," Karen said. "I had hoped he'd be here today, but I wasn't able to get hold of him."

"Typical!" someone shouted.

"To be fair," Karen said. "I don't think the fault lies with Kelvin."

"They're all crooks!" an irate young man shouted.

"You may be right," Karen conceded. "I don't know. None of us do."

"What about the other end of the operation?" I asked.

"That's run by two vampires. I don't know anything about them. Do you think you'll be able to help us?"

"I hope so. Before I leave today, I'd like to speak to a few more of you, to gather as much information as I can about Hauntings Unlimited."

"Thanks, Jill. I'm sure everyone will be more than happy to talk to you."

Chapter 14

All of the ghosts in the hall were eager to tell their stories, all of which ran along similar lines. They'd all been paid initially, but after one, two, or for a few of the more fortunate ghosts, three months, the payments had stopped. They were then strung along and fed all manner of excuses for the 'delayed' payments. Eventually, the ghosts would tire of working for no pay, and throw in the job.

At first, I struggled to make sense of what was happening. If Hauntings Unlimited were out and out fraudsters, why pay at all? Why stop after a month or two? But then I realised that this was in fact quite a clever con. Every ghost recruited by the company ended up working several months for free. The company didn't care if the ghosts eventually got fed up and left because there were plenty of others waiting to take their place. Assuming that the company was being paid for every ghost/month, but only passing on a fraction of that money, they would be able to skim off as much as half of the money received. Given the number of ghosts hired by Hauntings Unlimited, that would add up to a pretty penny, over time.

Now I knew how the scam worked, the question was: who was taking the money? The obvious suspects were Kelvin Toastmaster, the ghost who ran the GT end of the operation, and the two vampires who handled the human end. Karen Coombes had tried to get Toastmaster to attend the meeting, but she had been unable to get hold of him. She did, however, have his office address, so while I was in GT, I decided to pay him a visit.

Toastmaster's office was in a run-down building not far from Spooky Wooky. There were dozens of small businesses based in the same building. As there was no central reception and no directory to show where any of the individual businesses were located, it took me almost fifteen minutes to track down Toastmaster Enterprises, which inevitably was at the end of the last corridor on the top floor of five.

"Yes?" the woman behind the desk barked. She was chewing gum while simultaneously eating an apple—quite a feat.

"I'd like to see Kelvin Toastmaster."

"Not in."

"When will he be in?"

"Don't know."

"Where is he?"

"Don't know."

Just then, I heard someone in the back room cough.

"Who's that?"

"Who's what?" She tossed the apple core into the waste bin at the other side of the room. Very impressive.

"I think Kelvin Toastmaster is through there." I gestured to the door behind her.

"I've already told you. He isn't here."

"In that case, you won't mind if I take a look."

She was too slow to block my path. By the time she was out of her chair, I was already through the door.

"Kelvin Toastmaster, I presume?"

"Lorna?" he yelled. "Why did you let her in?"

"Sorry, Kelvin. She just barged in."

"Thank you, Lorna. You've been very helpful." I shut the door in her face.

"Who are you?" Toastmaster demanded. He was the first ghost I'd met in GT that actually looked like a ghost. Or at least how I'd always assumed a ghost would look. He was incredibly pale—bordering on albino.

"I'm Jill Gooder."

"You're that witch. I've heard about you. What do you want with me?"

"Just a chat."

"What about? I'm a busy man."

"So I see." I glanced at the paperback novel that was open on his desk. "I want to talk to you about how Hauntings Unlimited are ripping off hundreds of people."

"That's not true, and anyway, what's it got to do with you?"

"I've been hired by the people who have been cheated out of their money, to find out what's going on."

"Okay. I'm sorry I was a little short, but I'm as frustrated by this situation as all those who have lost money. This problem makes my job much more difficult because I'm having to recruit more and more ghosts, and as word about the non-payments spreads, that becomes more difficult."

"Are you saying that the problem lies with the vampires who are running the human end of the operation?"

"I don't know. I just know it isn't me."

"Have you confronted them?"

"Of course. They blame the customers who are using our services. They maintain that we're not being paid by the humans."

"Do you believe them?"

"I don't know what to believe. I'm caught in the middle."

"Someone, somewhere is stealing this money, and I intend to find out who it is."

"Well, it isn't me."

"It had better not be because if it is, you'll be seeing me again, and next time, I won't be in such a good mood."

***

I wasn't sure I believed Toastmaster, but I had no proof that he was the one pocketing the money. According to him, the vampires blamed the human customers for non-payment. That simply didn't ring true. While there might be a few bad payers, that alone wouldn't account for the scale of the problem. I needed a different approach, and I had already come up with a plan, but before I could put it into action, I would need to get hold of the colonel. I tried phoning him, but my calls just rang out, so I popped back into Spooky Wooky, and asked the guys there to get the colonel to contact me the next time he came into their tea room.

I'd been so busy that I hadn't yet got around to following up Anthony Coultard's report about the starlight fairy wings. If what he'd said was true, I had to do something to put an end to that awful trade.

Back in Washbridge, I found the shop that Coultard had mentioned to me. Shiny Shiny was anything but. Grotty Grotty would have been a much more appropriate name. The small shop sold all manner of cheap jewellery and tacky trinkets. It didn't take me long to spot the display of fairy wings.

"Lovely, aren't they?" The old woman behind the

counter had only two teeth: one in her top jaw, one in the bottom. "Real fairy wings, they are." She cackled.

The woman wasn't a witch, but she was more like the fairy tale version of one than any of the real ones I knew (except for Grandma, of course). The wording on the display read: 'Real Fairy Wings'. The sad irony was that the humans who bought them would assume that was simply a marketing gimmick. As far as they were concerned, fairies weren't real. Not for one moment would any of them realise that real fairies were being murdered for their wings.

"How much are the fairy wings?"

"Twenty pounds a pair. Three pairs for fifty quid."

"I like these. The yellow and white marble-effect ones. Do you have any more like these in different colours?"

"Nah. That's all we've got until our supplier comes again."

"When will that be?"

"Next Tuesday."

"What time?"

"He usually comes around eleven o'clock."

"Okay, I'll pop back after then."

"Do you want to take the yellow ones for now?"

"I can't. I don't have enough money on me."

***

My next port of call was WashBets.

"Hi, Tonya."

"How do you know my name?"

"It's on your badge. Just so you know, I don't have a complaint, so I don't need to see Bryan. I'm not Ryan's girlfriend, but I would like to speak to him about Megan who *is* his girlfriend."

I could almost see the cogs in her brain processing that information.

"So, you don't have a complaint?"

"Correct."

"And you aren't Ryan's girlfriend?"

"Also correct."

"And you want to see Ryan about Megan who *is* his girlfriend?"

"Bingo!" It had taken me a while, but I'd finally solved the enigma that was Tonya.

"What's your name?"

"Jill Gooder. I'm the one who got you and Norman together."

"Who's Norman?"

It had been going so well, too.

"Nice to see you, Jill." Ryan greeted me with a smile. "You spend more time in here than a lot of our regulars."

"Not through choice."

"I assume there's another problem."

"I wouldn't be here otherwise. I'm going to ask you a question, and I need an honest answer."

"Okay."

"I'll know if you're lying."

"I won't. I promise."

"Have you tried to turn Megan?"

The look of outrage on his face told its own story. "No! I love her. I would never, ever do that. Why would you even think it?"

"She told me that she's recently had the urge to bite

someone's neck—to taste their blood. She actually asked me if I thought she was turning into a vampire."

"Are you being serious? This isn't some kind of wind-up, is it?"

"I'm deadly serious, but I did try to calm Megan down by making it into a joke."

"Did it work?"

"Yeah. Megan seemed to realise how ridiculous she was being. Or at least, how ridiculous she *thought* she was being."

"It must be the synthetic blood," he said.

"Could it have this effect?"

"I don't know. It was never meant for human consumption."

"I think you're probably right."

"I'll have to find somewhere else to store it. I have friends who live in the same apartment block. I can get them to hold onto it for me until I come up with a more permanent solution."

"What will you tell Megan when she asks why you aren't drinking it any longer?"

"I'll—err—I don't know."

"Why don't you tell her that you've read a report that said the supplement caused side effects?"

"What kind of side effects?"

"I don't know. Body odour, an increase of body hair, anything so long as it ensures she doesn't press you to buy any more."

"Okay. I'll come up with something. Thanks again, Jill."

"No problem."

***

On the way back to my office, I walked past a small toy shop. Something in the window display caught my eye, so I nipped inside.

"How much are those?"

"The rubber-sucker dart guns?" The roly-poly man behind the counter took them out of the window. "Seven pounds."

"Can't I just buy one?"

"Sorry. They come in pairs."

"Okay. I'll take them."

The outer office was still more jungle than workplace.

"Hello?" Mrs V shouted.

"It's me. I'll be with you in a moment." Once again, I followed the right-hand path to her desk. "Did you get hold of Mr Greenfinger, and ask him to get these moved?"

"I have some bad news about that."

"Oh?"

"It seems Rodney put his back out carrying all of these up here. He's laid up in bed and can't move. He apologised for going over the top, but couldn't say when he'd be well enough to come and get them. I'm really sorry about this, Jill."

"Me too."

"I may be able to help," Winky said, after I'd eventually fought my way through the foliage to my office.

"Help with what?"

"To get rid of all those plants out there."

"Really? That would be great."

"It'll cost you, though."

"Doesn't it always? How much this time?"

"There's an awful lot of them."

"I can't afford to pay very much."

"Thirty pounds the lot."

"Twenty."

"Twenty-five."

"Deal. But you'd better leave a couple in there because I promised Mrs V could have some in the office."

"Hand over the cash now, and the plants will be gone by Monday morning."

"Okay." I gave him the money. "You'd better not let me down."

"My word is my bond."

I took the toy guns out of my bag, and ripped open the packaging.

"Those won't scare the bad guys." Winky scoffed.

"They're not supposed to. They're to help me to practice for paintball."

"I can give you lessons, if you like?"

"What do you know about guns?"

"I just happen to be an expert marksman."

"Of course you are." I slipped one of the guns into the drawer in my desk, and put the other back in my bag. "I think I'll pass."

"Your loss."

"How did the choir competition go?"

"I don't want to talk about it."

"I take it you didn't win?"

"We were disqualified."

"Why?"

"I'd rather not say."

"You might as well tell me. I won't let up until you do."

"If you must know, I failed the drug test."

"They have drug tests at a choir competition?"

"Yes. There have been several cases of competitors using magic formulas to enhance their vocal chords."

"How come you failed the test?"

"It must have been that stupid throat syrup. I had no idea that would cause me to test positive."

"Didn't you explain what had happened?"

"I tried to, but they wouldn't listen. I've been banned for the next two years."

"That's very harsh."

I tried to appear sympathetic, but inside I was celebrating the fact there would be no more 'Do, Re, Mi, Fa, Sol, La, Ti, Do'.

Just then, the colonel appeared.

"Harry at Spooky Wooky told me you wanted a word."

"Yes. Thanks for dropping by."

"No problem. Cilla is having her nails done, so I was at a loose end anyway. What can I do for you?"

"I'm on the trail of some conmen, but I really need the use of a country house, and I wondered if there was any way I might be able to use your old place?"

"If it was up to me then I'd say 'yes' straightaway, but of course there's the current owner to consider. Will you need it for long?"

"Not really. A couple of hours should do the trick, provided you can give me at least twenty-four hours' notice."

"Leave it with me. I'll keep my ear to the ground. If I hear there's going to be a suitable window, I'll call you on the old blower."

"Great! Thanks, Colonel."

Chapter 15

There was shouting coming from the outer office:
"Hello? Anyone there?"
"Over here?"
"Where?"
"Follow the path."
"Which one?"
"The one on the right."

Oh boy!

It sounded like we had a visitor. If it was a potential client, what kind of first impression would they get from the jungle?

Mrs V came through to my office. "There's a Mr Wragg out there. He says he'd like to see you, but I think he might be drunk."

"Is he being rude or abusive?"

"No, nothing like that. He's just rather unsteady on his feet; he keeps wobbling around."

"Maybe he got disorientated having to find his way through the jungle?"

"I don't think it's that. Shall I tell him that you're too busy to see him?"

"No. I can spare a few minutes. Show him in."

Mrs V hadn't been exaggerating. The man did indeed seem very unsteady on his feet; his whole body seemed to sway from side to side. He was dressed rather strangely too—in a long coat, which had a deep hood that hid his face.

"What can I do for you Mr Wragg?"

"Just a moment, please."

He took off the hood, and threw open his coat, and then everything became clear. The reason he appeared to be unsteady on his feet was that Mr Wragg wasn't a human. He was in fact a pixie. Or, to be precise, ten pixies, all standing on each other's shoulders.

I was speechless.

What? It does happen occasionally.

"Okay, boys. Down you get." The topmost pixie jumped down; the others followed his lead.

"I'm guessing you aren't really Mr Wragg." I addressed the pixie who had played the 'head'.

"My name really is Wragg. Colin Wragg. I apologise for the subterfuge, but it's the only way that we pixies are able to move around the human world unnoticed."

"I understand, and I apologise for the jungle outside."

"No problem. I should introduce my colleagues. From left to right, they are: Tommy, Arthur, Donny, Mark, Charlie, Gordon, Albert, Jimmy and Johnny.

"Hi, guys. I'm probably not going to remember all of your names. What can I do for you all?"

Colin stepped forward. He had obviously been nominated to head the delegation.

Head the delegation. Get it? Come on. What's the point of my coming up with all of this good stuff if it's going to go straight over your head?

"The king of the pixies has asked us to get in contact with you. He needs your services."

"I'm honoured, but why me?"

"He heard of the excellent work you did in closing down the BeHuman operation, and wondered if you could help him."

"With what exactly?"

"It's a matter of some sensitivity that he'd prefer to discuss face-to-face. Would you be able to visit him at his palace?"

"Right now?"

"No. He has important business all day today. He was hoping you might be able to come over on Monday, if that's convenient?"

"Certainly."

***

Not long after Mr Wragg and the other nine pixies had left, I had a phone call from Grandma, asking me to go down to Ever.

"Was that man drunk?" Mrs V asked, as I was on my way out.

"No. Just a little unsteady on his feet." All twenty of them. "I'm going down to Ever."

"Ask your grandmother what she intends to do about our broken knitting needles, would you?"

"Will do."

There was no sign of Kathy, but Maria was busy in the tea room. She looked stunning in her red trouser suit.

Okay, I'm lying. Those Everette outfits were truly awful.

"Hi, Maria."

"You didn't warn me about this." She gestured to her outfit.

"Sorry. I had no idea this change was on the cards. Are you going to stick around?"

"I'm not sure. I don't want to make any rash decisions until I'm over the initial shock."

"What did Luther make of your outfit?"

"He thought it was sexy."

"Really?"

"No, of course not. He couldn't stop laughing. Did you want something to eat or drink, Jill?"

"No. I'm here to see Grandma."

"When you warned me how bad she could be, I thought you were exaggerating."

"I wasn't."

"I know that now. This morning, she asked me if I knew anything about the treatment of bunions."

"What did you say?"

"Nothing. I just got out of her office as quickly as I could."

"Very wise."

Grandma was in her office, reading The Bugle.

"I didn't know you read that rag."

"I don't. I was just checking my horoscope."

"You surely don't believe in that rubbish? What does it say?"

"That a close relative is going to do the charitable thing, and come to work for me."

"See. That just proves my point. Total garbage. What did you want to see me about?"

"I've worked out which kind of spell Ma Chivers has embedded into the free knitting needles. It's a 'mind control' spell."

"That sounds like bad news."

"It is. When she activates it, she'll be able to control all of those who have the knitting needles."

"To what end?"

"That, I don't know, but I doubt it will be anything good."

"What about Mrs V and Jules? Will they be okay?"

"Yes, thanks to me. Breaking the needles, breaks the spell."

"Then that's what we'll have to do. We have to break all of the needles."

"That's an ingenious plan. And how, exactly, are we going to track down everyone who has received a free pair of needles?"

"I hadn't thought that far ahead."

"Clearly not. The only way we can thwart her plan is to get her to take a spell-blocker potion."

"How would that work?"

"It's very complicated, but essentially it will stop her from activating the spell which she's embedded into the needles. I can prepare the necessary potion, but then somehow we need to get Ma Chivers to drink it."

"How long will it take you to prepare the potion?"

"It's not something that can be done quickly. If I get onto it straightaway, I should have it finished by Monday."

"That long? What if she decides to activate the 'mind control' spell before then?"

"We'll just have to hope she doesn't."

"Okay. When the potion is ready, let me know, and I'll make sure she drinks it."

"How are you going to manage that?"

"Let me worry about that."

***

I was ready for a drink and something to eat, so I magicked myself over to Cuppy C. Much to my surprise, Aunt Lucy was behind the counter.

"What are you doing in here?"

"The twins roped me in. They're both so taken with the pups that they wanted another day off. That would have left them short-handed in here today, so they asked if I'd mind covering for them."

"They should have given me a call. I could have helped out for a few hours."

"That's what I suggested to them, but they said—err—that you were probably too busy."

"What did they really say? It's okay. I can take it."

"I don't like to say."

"Come on. It's nothing I haven't heard before."

"They said you were a liability behind the counter, but I'm sure they didn't mean it."

"I'm sure they did. It's okay. I can't say I miss working behind that counter. Have you been busy?"

"Not particularly. I'm due for a break. Why don't I join you? What are you having? Your usual?"

"Is Christy's bakery back in business?"

"Yes. They're fully operational again now."

"Great. In that case, I'll definitely have my usual, please."

Aunt Lucy got one of the other assistants to cover for her, and then she came to join me. Needless to say, the muffin was every bit as delicious as usual.

"How's the P.I. business, Jill?"

"Busier than I can remember. I'm working on a very

strange case in the human world. Perfectly normal, healthy young women are going insane overnight for no apparent reason."

"How terrible."

"It is. Plus, I'm working on a case for a number of ghosts in GT who have been cheated out of their wages. And, earlier today, I was visited by a delegation of pixies who have requested I visit their king early next week. It appears there's something he needs my help with."

"You really are busy. I don't know how you do it. You'd better have another cake, to keep your strength up."

"Go on then. But only because you're twisting my arm."

***

I hadn't fed Winky since that morning, so I thought I'd better drop in at the office before heading home. After walking along the now familiar path through the jungle, I found a message scribbled on a slip of paper on Mrs V's desk. The message read: *There are no messages.*

When I went through to my office, I got the shock of my life. Seated on the sofa was an old man—he was seventy if he was a day. He was wearing an eye patch, and was eating salmon straight from the tin. There was a newspaper open on the sofa beside him, and he appeared to be checking the racing results.

"I knew I should have bet on the favourite," he grumbled to himself.

"Excuse me! What do you think you're doing?"

"Just checking my bets. I knew I should have put a fiver on Freddy's Dream."

"Never mind Freddy's Dream. You're trespassing. This

is my office."

He laughed. "You don't know who I am, do you?"

"No. I've never seen you before in my life."

"We see each other most days. Most weekdays, at least."

"I think I'd know if I'd seen you before."

"My name is Walter, but you know me as Winky." He laughed again.

"Did you just say — ?"

"Winky, yes. I told you the other day that I was really a shape-shifter. Didn't you believe me?"

I had to lean back against my desk, otherwise I would have collapsed. "You're not seriously telling me that you're my cat?"

"That's precisely what I'm telling you."

"And that you've been living in this office with me all this time, and I had no idea that you were really — ?"

"Walter. That's right."

"I don't know what to say."

Just then, someone laughed. The sound came from under the sofa. Moments later, Winky — the real one — came rolling out. He was laughing so hard that he had to hold his sides.

"Sorry, Walt." He managed eventually. "I tried to hold it in, but that was sooo funny."

"I knew that it was a trick all along," I said.

"No, you didn't." Winky wiped tears from his eye. "You fell for it hook, line and salmon."

"I'm going home." I started for the door.

"Priceless!" Winky shouted after me. "I'm so glad I got it on video."

"And you laughed at me when I was practising for the egg and spoon race?" Jack scoffed.

I'd lined up some empty boxes at one end of the table, and was trying to knock them over with the darts from my toy gun.

"This is different."

"How is it different?"

"Egg and spoon is a joke, but paintball is deadly serious. We can't let Kathy and Peter win."

"You're useless." He laughed. "You haven't hit one of those boxes yet."

"There must be a draught in here which is taking the darts offline."

"Here. Let me have a go."

He knocked the box over with his first shot.

"No one likes a show-off."

Chapter 16

"Hey! Do you mind?" Jack ducked just in time. "That nearly hit me."

The rubber-sucker dart had almost grazed his head before it stuck onto the fridge door.

"You were standing in front of my target."

"Why did you put the target on the fridge? I need the milk."

"Hurry up, then. You're costing me valuable practice time."

"Don't you think maybe you're taking this a little too seriously? It's only a game."

"Paintball is not a game! It's deadly serious. This is you and me versus Kathy and Peter, and losing isn't an option."

"Thank goodness you're not competitive, or you'd be unbearable. Incidentally, have you seen the weather?"

I'd been so busy practising that I hadn't even looked out of the window.

The rain was bucketing down.

"How long has it been doing this?"

"Most of the night. I'm surprised you didn't hear it. It's going to be pretty muddy."

"We'll just have to finish them off quickly, then."

Kathy and Peter had been watching for us through their front window. Peter made a dash for our car; Kathy put up an umbrella, and walked down the drive.

"Shall we go bowling instead?" she said.

"I'd be up for that," Jack quickly agreed.

"No!" I objected. "We're going paintballing. That's what

we agreed. And besides, we've already paid."

"I thought you'd be the first to want to cancel," Kathy said. "You hate it when it's muddy."

"This is different."

"Jill's been practising non-stop for the last couple of days." Jack grinned.

"No, I haven't. It was only a few minutes here and there."

"Why don't we go to the paintball place, and see if it's even open?" Peter, ever the sensible one, suggested. "It might be closed because of the weather."

That's what we did, and when we arrived at Red Strike Paintball, we were in for a bit of a surprise.

"Look at the sign." Jack pointed. "They have an outdoor and an indoor course. Which did you book, Peter?"

"I don't know. Outdoor, I think. Let's go inside and see what they say."

It turned out that we were booked on the outdoor course, which was still open despite the weather. Even so, they gave us the option to swap to indoor because no one had booked that slot.

"I vote for indoor," Kathy said.

"Me too." Jack raised his hand.

"And me." Peter did the same.

"Whatever." I shrugged. "It makes no difference to me. It isn't going to take long for us to finish you off either way."

"You're very sure of yourself, aren't you?" Kathy said.

"Very. We're going to take you two down, no problem."

"Do you want to put your money where your mouth is?" Kathy challenged. "How about a fiver?"

"Make it a tenner."

"You're on."

We were shown to the changing rooms where we put on the one-piece camouflage suits; they were not very flattering. Next, we were issued a helmet, and face mask.

"Welcome to Red Strike Paintball," the man in charge said. "Have any of you played before?"

Played? He made it sound like it was some kind of game. Didn't he realise how serious this was?

None of us had 'played' before, so he ran through the rules. Boring! Rules are for losers.

"If you get hit, you're out. Okay?"

We all nodded.

"The last team standing is the winner. Any questions?"

"What's the record for the fastest win?" I asked.

"I have no idea." He seemed surprised by the question. "Seeing as you've decided to play as teams, two of you should enter the door marked 'A' over there. The other two should enter through door 'B'."

"We'll be the A-Team," I said.

"You can pick up your guns and ammo belt just inside the door. They must not be taken out of that room. Understood? Good. Okay then. Off you go. You have until one team wins, or thirty minutes, whichever is the sooner."

"Five minutes should be long enough," I said, as I led Jack to door 'A'.

Inside the room was a maze of walls and rocks, constructed from a mix of wood and plastic. The floor was covered in artificial turf. Jack and I grabbed our guns and ammo, and then dived for shelter behind a low wall. We couldn't see Kathy or Peter from where we were, but I could hear muffled voices coming from the far side of the room.

"You flank left, and I'll flank right," I whispered.

"I thought we'd stay together."

"Those are loser's tactics. That's exactly what Kathy and Peter will do, but we'll be waiting for them, and take them by surprise."

"Are you sure that will work?"

"Of course I am. I'm going to make a dash for that next wall over there. Cover me."

"Cover you? Oh? Err—okay."

"I'm relying on you. As soon as I break cover, I'll be vulnerable, so you need to lay down covering fire. Got it?"

"Covering fire? Err—yeah. Got it."

He wasn't exactly filling me with confidence, but I was fairly sure the opposition were not close enough to do any harm, so I was prepared to take the risk.

"On one." I raised three fingers. "Three, two, one!"

I broke cover, made a dash to the next wall, and dived down behind it.

"Now you!" I half-mouthed, half-gestured to Jack.

I counted him down, and then readied my gun in case I caught sight of either Kathy or Peter. On my signal, Jack made a rush for the wall located at the opposite side of the room from where I was now positioned. So far, so good. When Kathy and Peter showed their faces, we'd take them by surprise, and annihilate them. That tenner was as good as mine.

Moments later, I heard footsteps, so I gestured to Jack to be ready. He gave me the thumbs up.

Kathy suddenly appeared from behind a wall, just in

front of Jack.

"Get her!" I yelled, and he opened fire.

What? You cannot be serious! What was that supposed to be? The paint pellets hit the floor and the wall, but went nowhere near Kathy, who ducked out of sight again.

I gave up my cover, and dashed over to join Jack.

"What were you playing at?" I yelled. "You had a clear shot."

"She took me by surprise. I didn't have time to line up my shot."

"You're supposed to be a policeman."

"I don't carry a gun. I've never fired one before."

"I told you that you should have practised."

Just then, I saw something move on the opposite side of the room. It was Peter, but he'd disappeared before I could get off a shot.

"I think I saw something." Jack stood up before I could stop him.

Two paint pellets exploded as they hit him in the back. I glanced over the top of the wall just long enough to see Kathy; she had a huge grin on her face.

"They got me." Jack slumped down.

"A lot of use you are. Looks like it's down to me."

I was on my own, and outflanked. If I took cover from Peter, I'd be open to a shot from Kathy, and vice versa. I'd been totally outmanoeuvred, and it was all Jack's fault. Any moment now, I'd feel the thud of a paint pellet, and it would be game over.

The only thing I could do was accept my fate, and take the defeat in good part.

What? Of course I'm joking.

I cast the 'sleep' spell on Jack, then made myself

invisible. Unseen, I crept from behind the wall, and positioned myself at a point midway between where Kathy and Peter were located. I watched as Kathy counted down on her fingers. On her signal, they broke cover, and charged towards the wall behind which they expected to find me, cowering.

I quickly reversed the 'invisible' spell, and now had them both in my sights.

"Surprise!"

Before they had chance to turn around, let alone get off a shot, I'd plastered them both with paint pellets.

"How did you get there?" Kathy stared in disbelief.

"What can I tell you? I'm a tactical genius."

"Well played, Jill." Peter was gracious in defeat.

"She cheated." Kathy fumed.

"How did I cheat? I just out-thought you. You aren't going to be a bad loser, are you?" I grinned. "That's ten pounds you owe me, loser!"

When we'd changed and were back in the car, Kathy was still moaning. "I still don't understand how you managed to get around the back of us. I would have seen you."

"But clearly you didn't. It's called stealth tactics. If you like, I'll give you some tuition before the next time we play."

"Who says we'll be playing again?"

"Surely you want to try to get your own back, don't you? We could make the wager twenty pounds next time."

When we dropped them back at their house, Kathy was still muttering under her breath about my underhand tactics.

"We'll see you both tomorrow for the barbecue," Peter said, as he got out of the car.

"What barbecue?" I asked Jack as we set off for home.

"Didn't I mention it? I thought seeing as how they were coming around to see the sandpit, we might as well make a day of it. I've invited a few of the neighbours too."

"Thanks for telling me."

"Sorry. I meant to mention it, but you've been so engrossed in your shooting practice, I didn't like to disturb you."

"All that practice paid dividends, didn't it?" I waved the tenner that Kathy had given to me.

"I still don't understand how you managed to beat the two of them. I thought you were cornered."

"If you hadn't decided to take a nap after you got shot, you would have seen."

"I don't know what came over me. One minute I was wide awake, and the next, I was out like a light."

"It's a good job I'm a master tactician. We should play again soon. It was fun."

Jack pulled up outside the corner shop.

"Why have you stopped here?" I said.

"I thought I'd get some pop for the kids for tomorrow. I haven't got any money with me, though. Do you have any?"

"No."

"What about the tenner you won off Kathy?"

"You can't have that. I'm going to frame it, and have a small plaque engraved. That way, I can show it to them every time they come over."

"Don't be ridiculous." He snatched the banknote out of my hand.

"Hey, come back here with my trophy."

Chapter 17

It was Sunday, which meant I didn't have to get up for work. It was such a fantastic feeling to realise that I could close my eyes, snuggle under the covers, and go back to sleep for as long as I liked.

"Jill! It's time to get up!"

"Go away, Jack. I'm asleep."

"Come on, lazybones."

"It's Sunday, in case you'd forgotten."

"It's the barbecue, in case *you'd* forgotten."

Oh no! The barbecue. I had forgotten, or at least I'd tried to.

"Is it still raining? If it's raining, we really should cancel it."

"The sun is shining; it's a clear, blue sky. The weather forecast says it's going to be like this all day. Come on! We have lots to do."

"How come *we* have lots to do? All I did was ask Kathy, Peter and the kids to come around to see the sandpit. You were the one who decided to invite the whole neighbourhood over for a barbecue."

"I haven't invited everyone. Just Jen and Blake, Tony and Clare and Megan and her boyfriend—what's his name?"

"Dracula."

"There's no need to be so bitchy, Jill. I'm sure he's perfectly nice. Now, are you going to get up or do I have to drag you out of there?"

"Why don't you get back into bed? I'll make it worth your while."

"Get up, now!"

Whatever happened to the romance?

Jack spent the whole morning running around like a headless chicken. I spent the whole morning making encouraging noises, in between yawns.

Megan and Ryan were the first to arrive, just before midday.

"We brought this for you." Ryan handed me a bottle.

For a horrible moment, I thought he'd brought a bottle of synthetic blood, but then I realised it was red wine.

"Thanks."

"Are we the first ones here?" Megan asked.

"Yeah. The others should be here soon. You're both looking well."

"No thanks to Ryan." She shot him a look.

"It's not my fault," he protested.

Megan turned to me. "I was doing really well with that iron supplement. I haven't felt so good in years, but now Ryan reckons we shouldn't take any more of it."

"I told you about the report, Megan," he said.

"How can an iron supplement be bad for you? What do you think, Jill?"

"Me—err—I guess I'd err on the side of caution. Better to be safe than sorry."

"I suppose you're right," she conceded, somewhat begrudgingly.

"It looks as though our other guests have arrived. I'd better go say hello. Why don't you go and get a drink?"

"Blake, Jen, glad you could make it."

"Long time, no see, Jill," Jen said.

"Blake tells me we'll be losing you soon. You're going to

run a pub, I hear?"

"Yes. We're looking forward to it, even if it is all rather sudden."

"We'll be sorry to see you go. I assume the 'For sale' board will be going up soon?"

"Actually, we've decided to follow Mrs Rollo's example," Blake said. "House prices are rather flat, so we're going to rent it out, for a year at least. Then we can review it."

"Plus, that would mean we have the option of coming back if the pub doesn't work out," Jen said.

"I'm sure it will work out just fine. I can picture you both behind a bar."

"We've already spoken to an agent, and he reckons there'll be no problem letting the house, so you could have a new neighbour in a week or so."

Just then, my phone rang. "Sorry, I have to take this. Why don't you go and get a drink?" I waited until they were out of earshot. "Grandma?" My initial thought was that she'd somehow heard about the barbecue, and wanted to know why she hadn't been invited.

"You need to get over here now," she snapped.

"I can't. I have a thing."

"Forget about your thing. This is important."

"We're having a barbecue. I can't just leave my guests."

"I'm at my house in Candlefield. If you magic yourself here and back, no one will even know you were gone."

"Okay. I'll be there in a moment."

"Jill!" Jack called to me as I made my way back to the house. "What time are Kathy and Peter coming over?"

"They said midday; they should be here anytime."

"Can you just keep an eye on the steaks for a minute? I

need to go to the loo."

"Sorry, I can't. I need to go too, and it's urgent." I dashed into the house before he had the chance to argue. Once inside, I hurried upstairs, squeezed through the spare bedroom door, and magicked myself over to Candlefield.

***

It wasn't often that I visited Grandma at her house. She'd sounded so desperate that I wondered if she might be ill.

She wasn't. She was in rude health, and as ugly as ever.

What? It's true.

"What is it, Grandma? What was so urgent that it couldn't wait?"

"Witchfinders."

"What about them?"

"I've heard that there's been a shake-up at the top. The head witchfinder, an old guy by the name of Cuthbert Hargreaves, has retired. Or, if the rumours are true, he's been forcibly retired."

"Where did you hear about that?"

"WOW."

"I only asked."

"That's where I heard about it. From WOW."

"What's Wow?"

"W-O-W. Witches of Washbridge."

"I'm still no wiser."

"WOW is a group of Washbridge witches who meet up on a regular basis to discuss all things witch-related. A sort of social club, if you like."

"How come I've never heard of it before?"

"Why would you have?"

"Let me think. Maybe because I'm a *witch* and I live in *Washbridge*."

"That may be so, but membership is by invitation only. Have you received one?"

"No. Who's responsible for issuing them?"

"The WOW committee."

"Is there anyone I know on the committee?"

"Apart from me, you mean?"

"You're on the committee?"

"The chairman, actually."

"So, how come you haven't invited me to join?"

"That would smack of nepotism. Anyway, we aren't here to discuss WOW. There are more urgent matters that require our attention. The guy who has taken over as the head of the witchfinders is called Rex Wrathbringer."

"That has to be a made-up name."

"It is. His real name is Rex Radish, but he changed it by deed poll."

"I can't say I blame him, but what does it matter to us who's in charge there?"

"It matters a lot. The new guy has something to prove, and if what I hear is true, he plans to make his mark by grabbing a number of high profile scalps. And you know who fits that bill, don't you?"

"Me?"

"And me. If his people can destroy either of us, it will be a feather in Rex's cap."

"Thanks for the heads-up. I'll keep my eyes peeled."

"You'll need to do a lot more than just *keep your eyes peeled*. According to what I hear, Rex is sending two or three new witchfinders to Washbridge. We need to find out who they are and when they're coming."

"And how are we supposed to do that?"

"*We* aren't. *You* are."

"How?"

"You're going to get your new buddy, Yvonne, to tell you, of course."

"You know Yvonne was a witchfinder?" I was stunned. "How do you know?"

"Because, my dear young lady, I'm not as green as I'm cabbage-looking."

Come to think of it, she did look a little like a cabbage — in profile, that is. Probably best not to mention it, though.

"When did you find out?"

"I knew as soon as I met her at that awful party."

"You never said anything."

"I did consider destroying her there and then, but I thought you and Jack might not appreciate that, so I made out like I didn't know. Anyway, it was obvious that she'd retired. I figured she'd want to keep on your good side, and might come in handy at some point. Looks like I was right."

"I'm not sure about this. Yvonne and I got off to a rocky start, but we're okay now. I don't think she'd appreciate — "

"Spare me the excuses. This is a matter of life and death. You don't have a choice; you have to do this! Have I made myself clear?"

"Crystal."

"Good. I suppose you'll be wanting to go back to your barbecue. The one you didn't invite me to."

"It's only for a few neighbours. The main reason we

decided to have one was so that Kathy's kids could see the new sandpit we had put in for them."

"I assume you've checked it for sand demons."

"Very funny." I laughed.

"I'm glad you think it's a laughing matter."

"I thought they were only found under the beaches."

"Says who? That's how it used to be, but there are so many people hunting for them now, that some have migrated to the human world."

"To the seaside resorts, surely?"

"Most of them, yes. But the others—"

"Sandpits? Oh no! I have to go!"

"Thank goodness you're back." Jack collared me as soon as I stepped out of the house. "Watch these steaks, would you? I'm bursting to go to the loo."

"I have to check the sandpit first."

"The sandpit is just fine. Now take this." He handed me the tongs, and then shot into the house.

Fortunately, there was no one in the sandpit yet, so I'd be able to check it out as soon as he got back.

"Auntie Jill!" Lizzie appeared around the corner of the house, pursued by another three kids: two girls and one boy. There was no sign of Mikey.

"Hi, Lizzie. Are these your friends?"

"Yeah. Mummy said they could come and play in the sandpit too."

"Right. Where's Mikey?"

"He's gone fishing with his friend. He said sandpits are just for babies, but they're not, are they?"

"Definitely not."

"Can we go in it now?"

"Of course, you can," Kathy said, before I had a chance to speak. She and Peter were standing behind the kids.

"Hold on! Wait!" I yelled at the kids—stopping them dead in their tracks. "I have to check something first." I handed the tongs to Kathy.

"What do you need to check?" She gave me a puzzled look.

"The—err—depth."

"Depth? It's not a swimming pool."

"I know, but it just occurred to me that I haven't checked how deep the sand is. I wouldn't want anyone to get sucked under." I jumped into the sandpit, and quickly cast the 'detect-a-sand-demon' spell. Much to my relief it came back as all clear. "It's fine, kids. Not too deep at all. In you get."

The kids whooped with excitement, and then jumped in. Jack had bought two buckets and spades because he'd been expecting only Lizzie and Mikey. Lizzie took charge of handing those out.

"Cindy and I get to have the spades first. Charlotte, you and David can have them in a few minutes."

Sheesh, she was just like her mother.

Meanwhile, back at the barbecue, Jack had taken command once again.

"Are you sure the sand depth is okay?" Kathy smirked.

"Sand depth?" Jack looked puzzled.

"Jill was worried about the depth of the sand, weren't you, Jill?" Suddenly Kathy's eyes widened, and I could see a look of horror on her face. My heart sank. Had the sand demon evaded me? Had it grabbed Lizzie or one of the other kids? "What are those?" Kathy pointed.

I spun around to find two man-sized crabs had

appeared in the garden.

"It's okay." I reassured her. "Those are our neighbours, Tony and Clare."

"Hi, everyone," Tony the crab said. "Thanks for inviting us. I hope you don't mind us coming dressed like this, but we have another cosplay con next weekend, and we thought this would give us a chance to try out our costumes."

"CrabCon?" I asked.

"CrustaceanCon, actually, but crabs are our favourites."

The look on both Kathy and Peter's faces was a picture.

"Grub's up!" Jack shouted, and everyone made their way over to the barbecue.

"Sorry about the weird neighbours," I whispered to Kathy.

"They probably say the same thing to their friends."

"Jack and I aren't weird."

"Jack isn't."

"Thanks. So, anyway, what about that paintball?" I grinned. "Did we whup your sorry backsides or what?"

"I still say you cheated."

"How?"

"I don't know. I haven't figured it out yet, but I will."

Good luck with that. Snigger.

Chapter 18

Jules was standing at the top of the stairs, outside the door to the outer office.

"Have you forgotten your key?"

"No. You can't go in there, Jill."

"Why not? What's wrong?"

"It's full of bugs."

"What do you mean? Let me take a look."

"No! Don't open the door."

I ignored her, opened the door, and stepped inside. And immediately wished I hadn't. The noise from their wings was deafening, and I could barely see through the swarm.

Of locusts.

I had two choices: turn back and retreat, or try to make it to my office. I decided to go for it, and ran at full pelt. The tiny creatures crashed against my face and body, and I could even feel them in my hair. For a moment, I wasn't sure that I was going to make it, but then I managed to grab the door handle, and escape.

My heart was still pounding as I rested with my back against the door. Thankfully, the locusts hadn't made it into my office. Apart from the few that I had to pick out of my hair, that is.

"Did I do a good job or what?" Winky was on the sofa, looking very pleased with himself.

"Are you responsible for this?"

"I can't take all of the credit. I did have some assistance from Bertie the Bug, but yes, it was my idea. Brilliant, don't you think?"

"Are you totally insane?"

"You said you wanted the plants gone, and now they're

gone. And don't worry, I didn't forget that you wanted to keep a couple." He pointed to the two pot plants next to my desk. "I brought those in here before Bertie released the locusts."

"There is of course one minor flaw with your plan."

"Oh? What's that?"

"You may have got rid of the plants, but now I can't get into the outer office because it's full of LOCUSTS!"

"I know a man who could get rid of those for you, but it will cost—" He ducked to avoid the stapler I'd launched at him. "Hey! That nearly hit me!"

"Come here. I'm going to kill you!"

"That's just ungrateful, if you ask me," he said, as he disappeared under the sofa.

After making a call to Bugs Vamoose, I braved another locust-run, to re-join Jules.

"Thank goodness you're okay, Jill. I thought the bugs had got you."

"There's a man coming to get rid of them. He should be here within the hour."

"That's quick."

"Only because I agreed to pay for their Superfast Express service. It's going to cost an arm and a leg."

"I've just had a horrible thought." The colour drained from Jules' face.

"What?"

"You don't think—" Her words drifted away as she stared at the office door.

"What is it, Jules?"

"You don't think Annabel is in there, do you?"

"Mrs V? No. Of course not. Why? Did she say she was

coming in today?"

"No, but then she rarely does; she just turns up—usually before I do. What if she went into the office, and those horrible things—" Jules buried her face in her hands. "What if they've eaten her?"

"I'm sure she isn't in there. I would have seen her. Wouldn't I?" Now I was really worried. What if the locusts had stripped Mrs V's body to the bone?

I made a call.

"Hello?"

"Mrs V? Thank goodness."

"Jill? What's wrong?"

"Nothing. We—err—nothing. I just thought I'd call to say good morning."

"Are you feeling alright, dear?"

"Yeah. I'm fine. See you later. Bye."

Jules and I breathed a joint sigh of relief.

"So? Where are they?" The Bugs Vamoose man was barely visible beneath the netting which covered his face.

"Through there." I pointed to the office door. "There are lots of them."

"And you're sure they're locusts? I don't get many callouts for locusts. It's mainly wasps or bees. Cockroaches too."

"They're definitely locusts. Can you handle those?"

"Of course."

"Will you have to kill them?"

"No. I'll just sing them a lullaby until they fall asleep. What do you think? Now, please stand back."

"How long will this take?"

"Not long, but you won't be able to use the office for

several hours afterwards. Any more questions before I start?"

"No. Thanks." Once he was inside, I turned to Jules. "There isn't much point in you hanging around. Why don't you take the day off?"

"Are you sure?"

"Yeah. Will you give Mrs V a call, please, and tell her not to come in today?"

"What shall I tell her if she asks why?"

"You might as well tell her the truth. And you can mention that we won't need Mr Greenfinger to remove the plants now."

***

Jules had left, and I was just about to go and get myself a coffee, when a young man came charging up the stairs.

"Wait! You can't go in there!" I yelled at him, as he reached for the door handle.

"Why not? I want to see that Gooder woman."

He was wearing jeans and a denim waistcoat. His arms were covered in tattoos—including one of a squirrel hammering nails into a coffin. And to finish off the look, he had a shaved head.

"I'm Jill Gooder."

"What's wrong with Andrea?"

"Andrea Teller?"

"Yeah. What's the matter with her? No one will tell me."

"Who are you?"

"I'm Charlie. Charlie Drudge. I'm her boyfriend. I want to know what's wrong with her."

"Did you know she was in Regent's Hospital?"

"Yeah. Someone said she'd gone crazy, but that's bull. She was fine the other day when she was with me."

"How did you get my name?"

"I spoke to Carl at Total Cuts. He said you'd been asking questions about Andrea. I want to know what's going on."

"Why don't you sit down?" I pointed to the stairs. "I'll tell you everything I know, which isn't very much."

"Why can't we go into your office?"

"I've got bugs."

"I work in security. I could sweep the place for you, if you like?"

"Not that kind of bug." I waved my arms up and down. "The flying, creepy-crawly type."

"Yuk!" He shuddered. "I hate creepy-crawlies."

We sat on the stairs, and I told him everything I knew.

"Is there anything I can do to help?" he said.

"Not that I can think of, but I'll keep you posted if I have any more news."

"Thanks, and I'm sorry for bursting in like that."

"No problem."

"Good luck with the bugs."

When Carl at Total Cuts had told me that Andrea's boyfriend had tattoos, piercings, and a shaved head, I'd been convinced he was talking about Billy Bhoy. That had led me to believe that Billy was the common factor between the two cases. I now realised that Carl had been talking about Charlie Drudge.

***

The other young woman whose details I'd obtained from Regent's Hospital was Carmen Rigby. Her file showed no next of kin, but it did include a contact name: Melissa Jones — her flatmate. When I called Melissa, she was at home and said I could pop straight over.

"Is there any news on Carmen?" she asked, once we were seated at her kitchen table.

"No new developments, I'm afraid."

"How come you're looking into Carmen's illness? Is something fishy going on?"

"I'm not sure, but she isn't the only young woman to be affected in this way."

"Does that mean it's a virus or something? Do you think I might get it?"

"I'm sure you'll be okay. There are only three cases so far."

"Only three that you know about."

"True. Have you known Carmen long?"

"We've been flatmates for about six years now. She's the sweetest person you could ever wish to meet."

"Her file doesn't list a next of kin?"

"She doesn't have one. She never knew her father, and her mother died a few years ago."

"What about siblings, grandparents? Aunts? Uncles?"

"No. There's no one else. If I was all alone in the world, I'd have a real chip on my shoulder, but Carmen was always happy. It doesn't seem fair that something like this should have happened to her."

"Had she complained of feeling ill before?"

"No. She was never ill — not even when she was. If I get a runny nose, that's good enough for a few days off work.

Not Carmen, though. If she broke both legs, she'd still crawl into work. She really enjoys the company of the other girls she works with."

"Where does she work?"

"In the black pudding factory. I don't know how she can work there. It would turn my stomach."

"How did the illness take hold?"

"It was really weird. One night, we're just sitting chatting as normal. The next day, she's turned into someone possessed. I thought she was messing around at first, but then she tried to scratch my eyes out. I had to lock her in the flat while I called the ambulance. I feel guilty for getting her put away, but what else could I do?"

I thanked Melissa for her time, and promised to let her know if I made any progress. One interesting fact that had emerged from our discussion was that Carmen also worked at the black pudding factory. Could that connection be important? It seemed unlikely because the third victim, Andrea Teller, didn't work there. Still, it couldn't hurt for me to talk to some of the people who worked alongside Jasmine and Carmen.

I made a call to Jules.

"Jill? Did you want me to come back in? I'm at the spa. Cindy and I were going to get a sauna."

"No, you're okay. Look, I'd like to speak with the people who know Jasmine and Carmen the best."

"Who's Carmen?"

"Carmen Rigby. She's in Regent's Hospital with the same symptoms as Jasmine. I thought you'd know her; she works at the black pudding factory too."

"She must have started after I left. Do you want me to

get you the names and contact details of their closest friends?"

"It would be quicker and easier if I could speak with them all at the same time. Maybe, you could organise it for me to meet them at the factory? I'd like to do it tomorrow or the day after if at all possible."

"Okay. I'll get Lules to arrange it."

"Great. Enjoy your sauna."

My phone rang; it was Grandma.

"I've got it," she said.

"Got what?"

"The thing I've been toiling over all weekend. The potion to stop Ma Chivers, of course."

"That's great."

"I'll bring it up to your office now."

"No. Don't do that. The office is infested with locusts."

"Should I ask why?"

"Probably best not to. I'll pop down to Ever first thing this afternoon to collect it."

"Are you sure you'll be able to get Ma Chivers to drink it? You can't afford to mess this up. We don't have time to brew anymore."

"Have I ever let you down before?"

"Would you like me to list all of the times? I could do it chronologically or alphabetically. Which would you prefer?"

"Neither, thanks. And you don't have to worry about the potion. I've got this one."

"I hope so, for all our sakes."

Chapter 19

I had an appointment with the king of the pixies, but as I had a little time to kill before that, I dropped in at Cuppy C first.

"Aunt Lucy? I thought you'd only agreed to cover for the one day?"

"I take it you haven't heard yet, then?"

"Heard what?"

"The twins are devastated. Their dogs have gone missing."

"The puppies? Both of them?"

"First thing this morning, Pearl called me in tears, and then a few minutes later, Amber did the same. They said they were going to get in touch with you."

"I haven't heard from them yet. Do they think someone has stolen them?"

"What other explanation can there be? Do you think you'll be able to get them back, Jill?"

"I'll need to talk to the twins, but I can't go over there just now because I have an appointment with the king of the pixies. Will you tell Amber and Pearl I'll get over to see them just as soon as I can?"

"I will. Thanks, Jill. Your usual, I assume?"

"Yes, please."

"How was your weekend?"

"Okay. We played paintball on Saturday. Jack and I whupped Kathy and Peter, so that was good. Then on Sunday, we had a barbecue, which wasn't quite so good."

"Why not?"

"I don't like barbecues at the best of times, but the worst part was trying to explain to Kathy why I had to stop the kids going into the sandpit. I could hardly tell her that I was searching for sand demons, could I?"

"Sand demons?"

"I probably shouldn't have mentioned it. Grandma asked me to keep an eye open for them at Candle Sands, and then she told me that some were now living in sandpits in the human world."

"Oh dear." Aunt Lucy began to laugh.

"It's not funny. They could have eaten Lizzie."

"If such things existed, they could."

"Don't they?"

"Grandma was winding you up."

"You mean to tell me that she made the whole thing up?"

"I'm afraid so. There's no such thing; there never has been."

"I'm going to kill that woman!"

***

King Dollop lived in a magnificent palace, aptly named Palace Dollop. As with all things pixie, the building was incredibly small, so I was forced to shrink myself in order to pay him a visit.

"His highness is expecting you." The courtier, dressed in a sparkly blue suit, came to collect me from the entrance hall. "Before I take you through to meet his royal highness, there are some things you need to know. It's important that the correct etiquette is observed. You may find some of this rather unusual because it is very different to the customs observed in the human world. I'm sure you understand."

"Yes, of course. I wouldn't want to do anything that might cause offence."

"The first thing you need to know is how you should address his highness."

"I assume I should call him *your highness*?"

"Goodness no. His staff, such as myself, address him as 'your highness', but honoured guests, such as yourself, should address him as Top Dollop."

"Sorry? Did you just say—"

"Top Dollop. That's right. It may sound a little informal, but I assure you that is what is required."

"Okay. If you're sure."

"When you're introduced to him, you must not curtsy."

"Should I bow?"

"Goodness no. You should raise your hand like this. The king will do the same, and slap your palm with his."

"You mean a high-five?"

"I understand that's what you call it in the human world, but here it has a more formal connotation. Would you like to practise? Pretend I'm the king."

"Okay." I raised my hand, and said, "Top Dollop."

"Almost, but you need to say, 'Goes it, Top Dollop?'"

"Goes it?"

"That's it. Try again."

I did, and this time the courtier seemed satisfied.

"Okay. Follow me. The king will see you now." He led the way through an enormous set of double doors into a huge stateroom. Our footsteps echoed as we walked across the marble floor towards the throne.

"Your highness." The courtier bowed. "May I present Jill Gooder."

When the king stood up, I stepped forward, raised my

hand, and said, "Goes it, Top Dollop?"

The king gave me a look which was a combination of anger and disbelief. I glanced at the courtier who seemed to deliberately avoid my gaze.

"I beg your pardon?" the king boomed. "What kind of disrespectful behaviour is this?"

"I — err — I'm sorry — sir — your highness. I was told — "

The king's face cracked and he doubled up with laughter. The courtier was in stitches too. I had no idea what was going on.

"Sorry, Jill," the king eventually managed. "Just my little joke. Don't blame Chambers. This was all my idea. You can't imagine how boring this job can be. I need to liven things up occasionally. Will you forgive me?"

"Of course." I smiled — as much through relief as anything else. "What should I call you? Your highness?"

"Nothing so stuffy. Call me Arthur. Now, let's have a cup of tea, and we'll get down to business."

Moments later, tea and pixie cakes were served; they were delicious.

"What I'm about to tell you, Jill, is strictly off the record." The king was speaking in a hushed voice, even though there was now no one else in the room.

"I understand."

"The Forever Candle has been in the palace grounds for as long as anyone can remember. It has magical properties that make it shine brighter than one thousand conventional candles. And, no matter how long it burns, it never gets any smaller. A few days ago, the candle went missing. Between you and me, I couldn't care less if I never saw it again. To most pixies, the Forever Candle is an important symbol, but to me, it's an eyesore which gives off quite an unpleasant odour. But that's all beside the point because if word were to get out that it was missing, there could be widespread panic. Rumour has it that if the Forever Candle is lost, the kingdom will crumble. All complete nonsense of course."

"How come word hasn't already got out?"

"As soon as its disappearance was noticed, the Fountain Court, where it is normally kept, was closed off. Only a small number of trusted employees are aware of what has happened. We should be able to get away with keeping the grounds and gardens closed for a few more days, on the pretence that essential maintenance work is being carried out. Any longer than that, and awkward questions will be asked. That's where you come in. I'm hoping that you will be able to track down and return the candle before it's too late."

"How did the thief remove it?"

"It wouldn't have been too difficult because that area is normally open to the public. The candle doesn't have any value as such, and certainly isn't the kind of thing that could be sold on the open market without drawing attention. For that reason, it was never felt necessary to provide security to protect it. It has, after all, been in that same location for hundreds of years."

"Where is the Fountain Court?"

"Outside. To the rear of the palace."

"Could I see it?"

"Of course. I'll get Chambers to take you there before you leave."

"Do you get many visitors?"

"Not inside the palace; that's strictly out of bounds, but the grounds and gardens, including the Fountain Court, are open for most of the year."

"I assume your visitors are all pixies?"

"Not at all. All manner of sups visit the grounds and gardens, which were designed with extra wide pathways to accommodate our 'bigger' guests. What do you think our chances of recovering the candle are? Should I prepare for the worst?"

"Not yet. I wouldn't want to build up your hopes too high, but I already have a hunch I'd like to follow up on."

"You do? Would you care to share your thoughts?"

"I'd prefer not to just yet, but I'm cautiously optimistic."

After we'd finished our conversation, the king summoned Chambers, and asked him to show me to the Fountain Court. The circular courtyard was bordered by a number of small fountains. In the centre of the courtyard was a structure which resembled a bandstand. In there, stood a plinth, on top of which was a golden candlestick.

"I'm sorry about earlier," Chambers said. "The king enjoys his practical jokes."

"That's okay. I assume the candle would normally be kept over there?" I pointed.

"That's right."

"How close to it can visitors normally get?"

"As close as they like. And until now, there's never been a problem."

I spent the next few minutes looking around the area.

"Okay. I think I've seen enough."

"Do you have any more questions for me?"

"No, thanks. I have everything I need."

It was time for another trip to the seaside.

***

The first time I'd been to Candle Sands, I'd travelled there by train. The second time, I'd taken Lester's car. This time I didn't have any time to waste, so I magicked myself there.

I landed on the cliff top, and was on my way to the lighthouse when I heard the shriek of young voices coming from below. Two very excitable youngsters were pulling their parents along the beach—obviously eager to show them something.

And that something was the same performing dog that we'd seen on our first visit to the resort. There was already a small crowd gathered around the wizard and his dog. But it wasn't the performing dog that caught my eye; it was the cage behind the deck chair. A cage which contained two small puppies.

I hurried down the path to the beach, and joined the crowd. The eager young dog was performing its tricks, much to the delight of the onlookers, but I was much more interested in getting a closer look at the puppies. They looked familiar—too familiar for my liking. The markings on the two dogs were identical in every way to those on the puppies that the twins had taken home with them. Something about this just didn't smell right.

I called Daze.

"Hi, Jill. It sounds windy where you are."

"I'm on the beach at Candle Sands."

"It's alright for some." She laughed. "Don't get sunburnt."

"I'm working on a case, actually. I was just wondering if

you maintain any kind of photo database of known criminals?"

"There is one, but as a rogue retriever, I only have access to records of those criminals who have been convicted of crimes in the human world. To do a search on the whole database, you'd need to speak to Maxine Jewell."

"I'd be wasting my time there. She still hates me."

"What's this all about?"

"I may be barking up the wrong tree, but I think there's something funny going on over here. I have a bad feeling about this one guy — he's a wizard, and I think he may be running some kind of scam. If I can snap a photo of him, will you run a check on him for me?"

"Sure. It might take me a short while to get back to you, though."

"That's okay. Thanks, Daze."

Lots of people in the crowd were taking photos of the performing dog, so it was easy for me to snap a photo of the wizard without drawing attention to myself. I sent Daze a text message with the photo attached, and then made my way back up the beach path to the lighthouse.

Maude O'Nuts answered the door. "Jill? I didn't expect to see you again so soon."

"Is Duncan in?"

"Yes. He's just having a cup of tea. Would you like one?"

"No, thanks. Do you think I could have a quick word with him in private?"

"Of course. I'll leave you two in peace. I have some ironing to do."

I waited until Duncan and I were alone, and then said,

"I know about the Forever Candle, Duncan."

"I don't know what you're talking about."

"In that case, you won't mind if I take a look up there, will you?" I started towards the stone spiral staircase that led up to the light.

"No! You can't go up there!" He moved to block my way.

"I know you stole the Forever Candle, and I understand why you did it. You should never have been put in a position where you were forced to raise funds yourself just to keep the light burning. But the Forever Candle is an important symbol to the pixies. If it isn't returned soon, it could have far reaching implications for the pixie people."

All the wind seemed to go out of him, and he slumped down onto the stone step. "How did you know?"

"It was a few things. The first time I visited Candle Sands, you were really keen for me to see the light, but then on my last visit, it was obvious that you didn't want me to go up there. Then there was the odour—I thought at first it was incense, but now I realise it was the candle. You've been forced to raise funds just to keep the light burning, but now it's on all the time—even in the daytime when it isn't needed. That didn't make any sense until I heard that the Forever Candle had been stolen. Then I remembered that Maude had told me you'd visited the pixie palace grounds on your recent trip to Candlefield."

"I didn't go there with the intention of stealing the candle. I didn't even know it existed until that day. But when I saw it, I realised that it would solve all of my problems. It's so very tiny, and yet so powerful. I don't know what came over me—I just popped it into my pocket. No one saw me—not even Maude. I'm really sorry. What's going to happen to me now? Will I go to jail?"

"Not if I have anything to do with it, but the final decision isn't mine. There's someone else I need to talk to."

"What about the candle? Do you want to take it back with you?"

"Yes, please."

"What should I do?"

"You sit tight until I return."

"I really am sorry about all of this."

"I know. Try not to worry too much. Everything's going to be okay."

Chapter 20

When I returned to the pixie king's palace, Chambers looked surprised to see me.

"Jill? Did you forget something?"

"No. I need to see the king again."

"He always takes a nap at this time of day, and he doesn't like to be disturbed."

"I don't think he'll mind this once." I took the Forever Candle out of my bag.

"You've found it already?"

"Do you think the king will see me now?"

"I'm sure he will. Please wait there for a moment."

Not long after Chambers had gone through to the stateroom, I heard the king bellow something, but then a few moments later, Chambers reappeared, and beckoned for me to go inside.

"Can this really be true?" The king looked half asleep.

"This belongs to you, I believe." I handed the candle to him.

"I'd heard you were good, but I had no idea you were this good. How did you manage to find it so quickly?"

"I'd like to claim it was down to brilliant detective work on my part, but the truth is it was pure luck."

"Who stole it? I'll have them locked up for a very long time."

"I'd like to discuss that with you, if you can spare a few minutes?"

"Why don't we talk about it over tea and cakes?"

Now there was a good idea, if ever I'd heard one.

The king listened intently as I told him all about the

Candle Sands lighthouse and Duncan O'Nuts' efforts to keep the light burning. I made sure to emphasise that Duncan had not planned the robbery, but had acted on impulse and out of desperation. I concluded by saying that I hoped the king would be able to see his way clear to showing clemency.

"I went to Candle Sands once as a young boy," the king said. "I remember being fascinated by the lighthouse. I'm appalled to learn that the current lighthouse keeper is having to fundraise just to keep the light on."

"Will you prosecute him?"

"Of course not. The man is a hero. What I will do, though, is to ensure that he never has to resort to fundraising again. From now on, he will be provided with enough candles every month to keep the light burning. Free of charge, obviously. I'll get Chambers on to it as soon as you leave."

"That is very generous, your majesty."

"Don't you mean, Top Dollop?"

***

After leaving the palace, I checked my phone, and found I had two messages. The first was from Aunt Lucy, to inform me the twins were now at her house. The other one was from Daze; she'd tried to ring me, and wanted me to call her back.

"Daze? I'm sorry that I couldn't take your call before. I was at the pixie king's palace."

"Really?" She laughed. "The circles you move in nowadays."

"It's a case I'm working on. Have you got something for

me?"

"I got a match on the photo. His name is Michael Finn. He has a number of convictions for committing fraud in the human world. His favourite scam was to sell dog-shifters—passing them off as cute puppies. He worked with two accomplices: Denny and Benny Loggins. The Loggins brothers are two of the most accomplished shifters in the business—they're able to fool humans and sups alike."

"They certainly had us fooled."

"The two of them would wait until their new 'owners' were asleep in bed, and then help themselves to jewellery, before doing a runner. Michael got to keep the cash that had been paid for the puppies; Denny and Benny kept the proceeds from the sale of the stolen valuables. They always targeted day-trippers at various seaside resorts—that way, when the puppies 'disappeared', the distraught owners only ever thought to search their local area. Meanwhile, the shifters made their way back to the seaside to re-join Michael. Often the jewellery theft wasn't noticed until sometime later."

"How did they get caught?"

"One of my colleagues cottoned on to their little scam, and they were locked away for five years here in Candlefield. According to the database, the three of them were recently released, but they're no longer permitted to travel to the human world."

"I think they've revived their routine, but are now operating here in the sup world. The twins bought two puppies last week, but both dogs disappeared over the weekend."

"Has any of their jewellery gone missing?"

"They didn't mention it."

"Get them to double-check. I'll have a word with Maxine Jewell. I think it's time she and her people paid Messrs Finn, Loggins and Loggins a visit. Thanks for the tip-off, Jill."

***

I really wasn't looking forward to this.

"How are the girls?" I asked Aunt Lucy.

"Not great. They're in the lounge."

Amber and Pearl were seated on the sofa; they both had red, puffy eyes.

"You have to find Tommy," Pearl pleaded.

"And Timmy," Amber said. "The poor little thing must be terrified."

"I'm afraid I have bad news for you about the puppies."

"Oh no!" Amber cried. "They're not dead, are they?"

"Tommy and Timmy are actually Denny and Benny. They're not puppies; they're dog-shifters."

"That can't be right!" Amber shook her head. "You must have made a mistake."

"We would have known," Pearl insisted.

"I'm afraid it's true. The three of them: Benny, Denny, and the wizard, Michael, have been running this same con for several years. They used to run it in the human world until they were arrested by the rogue retrievers. They've recently been released from jail, and have obviously decided to target sups this time. I'm really sorry, girls."

"You mean to tell me that when I was cuddling Timmy, I was really cuddling some horrible man?" Amber shuddered at the memory.

"I'm afraid so."

"That's gross! I let him lick me on the face."

"I'm afraid I have more bad news. The *puppies* usually steal jewellery from their owner's houses before they do a runner. You'd better get back home and check if anything is missing."

"That's just great!" Pearl was no longer upset; she was angry.

"Maxine Jewell should already be on her way to arrest them, so there's a chance they won't have fenced any of your jewellery yet. I'm really sorry to be the bearer of such bad news."

"It isn't your fault, Jill," Amber said. "How did you work it out?"

"I had to make another visit to the lighthouse. While I was there, I spotted the wizard on the beach. He had the performing dog with him, and the cage with two cute puppies in it. Puppies that looked identical to those you took home."

"I'll murder them if I ever get my hands on them," Pearl grumbled, as she and Amber headed out the door.

"Poor girls," Aunt Lucy said. "They were so fond of those puppies. How did you get on at the pixie king's palace?"

"Very well. Case sorted."

"That was quick! It sounds like you deserve a muffin."

"Normally, I'd snatch your hand off, but I'm full to bursting with pixie cakes."

***

"Jill!" Kathy called to me as I hurried through Ever.

"Sorry, can't stop. Grandma is expecting me, and I'm already late."

"Okay. I'll catch you on your way out."

"You said you'd be here first thing this afternoon." Grandma put down her cocktail, and then tapped her watch. "It's almost midnight."

"It's just gone two. I'm sorry, but I've been run off my feet all day."

"Don't give me your sob stories. I have enough of my own. According to your sister and her buddies out there, I need to hire more staff. The youngsters of today just can't handle hard work."

"You could always go out there and help them."

"And who would do the strategizing then?"

"Does the cocktail help with that?"

She ignored the jibe, and took a tiny bottle from the top drawer of her desk. "Be careful with this. Don't drop it, whatever you do."

"Don't worry." I slipped it into my pocket. "I'll be careful."

"How are you going to make sure Chivers drinks it?"

"Let me worry about that. What happens after she does?"

"I mixed a 'bounce-back' spell in with the potion."

"What does that do?"

"When she tries to activate the 'mind control' spell, it will trigger the bounce-back, and—err—well, that would be telling."

"Come on, Grandma. Tell me."

"No. You'll just have to wait. It will be worth it, though. I promise."

"That was a quick visit," Kathy caught me on the way

out.

"I hear you've asked Grandma for more staff."

"Dead right, we have. This is the first time it's been quiet all day. My feet are killing me. I wish I had your job; you get to do what you want, when you want."

"Oh yeah. My job's a breeze."

"What's all this I hear about locusts?"

"Locusts?"

"Your grandmother said that your office had been infested by them?"

"That's ridiculous." I laughed. "She must have misheard or misunderstood. What I actually said was—err—that we had been *tested* for—err—*low cuss.*"

"What's cuss?"

"It's kind of a Zen thing. Cuss is good energy, so you need high levels of it. I wanted to make sure that our cuss levels weren't low, so I had it tested. I told Grandma we'd been *tested for low Cuss.* She must have thought I said we'd been *infested by locusts.* It's an easy mistake to make."

By now, Kathy looked thoroughly confused.

"Sorry, I really do have to run."

***

Although I'd told Grandma that there would be no problem administering the potion to Ma Chivers, I didn't actually feel as confident as I'd made out. The truth was, I was simply playing a hunch. I'd seen Ma Chivers send Cyril out for coffee from Coffee Triangle, and I'd heard her say that she needed her caffeine infusion at hourly intervals.

"You're Jill Gooder, aren't you?" the barista said.

"That's right."

"I thought so. You won the 'guess how many marbles are in the jar' competition."

"I did."

"We were supposed to take a photograph of the winner, to put in the paper."

"You can take one now, if you like."

"The bosses want a photo of you with your prize. With the giant triangle."

"It's at home. You can hardly expect me to bring it all the way back here just so you can take a photograph."

"Of course not. Someone could come out to your house, and take a photo there."

"Err — yeah. That sounds great. Why don't I give you a call later to arrange something?"

"Okay, thanks."

Don't hold your breath.

I found a seat close to the entrance, so I could keep a lookout for Cyril. After no more than thirty minutes, he came through the door. I waited until he was at the counter, then went over to stand behind him.

"Yes sir?" the barista said. "What can I get for you?"

"Flat white, please. Large."

"Hello, Cyril." I tapped him on the shoulder.

He spun around. "What do you want?"

"Yuk!" I pulled a face.

"What's up?"

"You've got something stuck between your two front teeth. Yuk, it looks horrible."

"Where?" He poked his teeth with his finger. "Has it gone?"

"No. Oh dear, it looks quite revolting."

He pushed past me, and headed to the toilet. As soon as he was out of sight, I grabbed his coffee, removed the lid, poured in the potion, and then replaced the lid.

"There's nothing there!" Cyril spat the words. "You want to watch who you mess with."

"Sorry." I held up my hands in mock surrender. "My bad."

Mission accomplished.

My phone rang; it was the colonel.

"Jill, I've just found out that Murray Murray will be out tomorrow afternoon. Is that any good to you?"

"I think so. I'll get in touch with Hauntings Unlimited to see if I can get them to pay me a visit then. I'll drop you a text later to confirm."

"No problem, Jill. Always happy to help."

Chapter 21

The next morning, I was up at the crack of dawn because I'd arranged to meet Lules and two of her work colleagues at the black pudding factory.

To my surprise, Jack was already up. He'd made breakfast for me — a full English, no less. There was a table cloth on the kitchen table — something we never did in the morning. In the centre of the table was a small vase with a single red rose in it. Next to my plate was a card and a small gift-wrapped present, tied with a pretty, pink bow.

Was it my birthday? No, that was ages yet. Christmas? Of course not. I might still be only half awake, but I would have remembered if it was Christmas day.

"Happy anniversary!" He gave me a peck on the cheek.

"Anniversary?"

"It's two years since we first met. You've forgotten, haven't you?"

"Don't be silly. Of course not. How could you even think such a thing?"

I cast the 'sleep' spell, steered him down onto the chair, and then gently lowered his head so it was resting on the table.

Quick, Jill, think! Where would be open at this time of the morning? The corner shop was open all hours, but they wouldn't have anything suitable. Unless—? No, a bucket didn't really fit the bill. Where else was open?

Then I remembered the large hypermarket, Sell-it-All, on the outskirts of Washbridge. Normally, I hated that place because it was always so busy, but surely not at seven o'clock in the morning. I rushed upstairs, showered, and got dressed. Then I magicked myself over to the store.

I made sure that I landed around the back so as not to scare any early morning shoppers.

Thirty minutes later, I was back at the kitchen table. Once I'd managed to catch my breath, I reversed the 'sleep' spell.

"I'll just go and get your card and present," I said.

"Huh?" Jack looked a little disorientated, and more than a little surprised when I produced a card and gift from the cupboard beside the sink.

"Happy anniversary." I gave him a kiss.

"I went in that cupboard earlier," he said. "I didn't see those."

"That's because you're half asleep. Are you going to open your present?"

"Err—yeah." He tore off the paper that I'd wrapped it in only a few minutes earlier. "A bowling shirt?"

"I wasn't sure whether to go for the red or the orange."

"This one is great. I love orange. Thanks." He looked at me, shook his head, and seemed even more confused.

"What's wrong?"

"When did you get dressed?"

"What do you mean?"

"When you came downstairs, you were still in your PJs."

"No, I wasn't."

"I was so sure."

"What did you get me?" I picked up the present, and tore it open. "This is gorgeous. Thank you."

"Do you like it?"

"I love it." I slipped the bracelet onto my wrist. "Give me a kiss. Happy anniversary, Jack."

"Happy anniversary, Jill. I guess this means that Kathy

owes me a fiver."

"How come?"

"She bet that you'd forget our anniversary."

"How could she ever think that? Just wait until I see her."

Snigger.

***

It was the first time I'd ever seen the black pudding factory, which was aptly named Black's Black Puddings. As arranged, Lules was waiting outside the gates; there were two other young women with her.

"This is Jill," Lules said. "I told you all about her."

"Hi, I'm Shelley."

"And I'm Shirley."

"Pleased to meet you both. I assume Lules has told you what this is about?"

"Yeah, I did," Lules said. "Shell and Shirl are friends with Jasmine and Carmen, aren't you, girls?"

"It's horrible what's happened to them," Shirley said.

"Scary too," Shelley chipped in. "Do you think it has something to do with the factory? I'm considering handing my notice in."

"A lot of the girls are thinking of leaving," Lules said. "This is scary stuff."

"I wouldn't do anything rash," I cautioned. "I don't think it's connected to the factory because I know of three cases in total, and one of them is someone who has no connection to this place."

"That's a relief," Shelley said.

"Not for poor Jasmine and Carmen!" Shirley snapped.

"That's not what I meant! You know I didn't mean that."

I didn't want this to descend into an argument, so I stepped in. "Before this happened, had either Jasmine or Carmen complained of feeling ill?"

All three women shook their heads.

"They were both as right as rain," Lules said. "Jasmine was stoked because she'd just started seeing someone."

"Billy?"

"Yeah. Have you met him? He's a sweet guy, despite the way he looks."

"He is and he's just as upset as you are. You're sure that neither of them was feeling 'off it' before they were struck down?"

"Positive," Shirley said. "The only problem Jasmine had recently was when she got that really bad toothache. Do you remember?"

Lules and Shelley nodded.

"It was Carmen who recommended her dentist to Jasmine," Lules said.

"How long ago was that?"

"Not long. Just a few days before she went off ill."

"I don't suppose you remember the name of the dentist, do you?"

"I have it." Shirley took out her phone. "I'm a bit fed up with my dentist, so I made a note of it, just in case I decide to swap. Here it is: Mr Dennis Tist."

A few minutes later, the three of them had to go into work, although none of them seemed particularly enthusiastic about doing so. I'd learned little of significance except perhaps for the dentist connection. Even that was very much a longshot, but before I dismissed it out of hand, I called Sarah Teller.

"It's Jill Gooder. How is Andrea?"

"Much the same I'm afraid. Have you made any progress with your enquiries?"

"Not really. Look, there's something I wanted to ask you. Had Andrea been to the dentist recently?"

"Yes, actually. She needed a filling. Why?"

"Which dentist does she go to?"

"She recently swapped dentists, so she could go to one closer to where she works. I've got a card somewhere. Can you hold on a moment while I find it?"

"Sure."

"Here it is. His name is Tist."

"Thanks."

This was suddenly looking much more promising. I called Carmen's flatmate, Melissa Jones.

"Melissa, it's Jill Gooder."

"Is there any news on Carmen?"

"No, sorry. Do you remember if Carmen had been to the dentist recently?"

"Yes. She went for a check-up. It was the day before she became ill. Why?"

"No reason. Thanks, Melissa."

Eureka. I had my connection!

***

I really wasn't looking forward to seeing the outer office. The locusts should be gone, but what of all the devastation left behind? The plants had all been stripped, but what was left of them would still take some clearing away. This was what came of being such a kind and considerate employer. I should have told Mrs V that I didn't want any plants in the office—that way, I would never have had any of these problems. I'm just too considerate and selfless; that's my problem.

What? Why are you laughing?

I braced myself, closed my eyes, and pushed open the door.

"Morning, Jill." Mrs V sounded much too chirpy, given the situation.

"Morning." I opened my eyes. And wow! There wasn't a plant or plant pot to be seen. The office was spotless. "Did you do this? It must have taken you ages."

"Do what, dear?"

"Tidy away all the dead plants and plant pots?"

"It was like this when I got here. I assumed that Rodney must have sent someone to collect them. Why did you say 'dead' plants?"

"Haven't you heard about the locusts?"

"What locusts?" She looked warily around the room. "I don't like creepy crawlies."

"Don't worry. They've all gone now. I do still have a couple of plants in my office. I'll bring them through in a few minutes."

"Alright, dear, and I'll make us a nice cup of tea. It sounds like you could do with one. Locusts?" She laughed.

"Oh, and Mrs V, would you make me an appointment at the dentist?"

"Toothache? I can't say I'm surprised, with all the muffins and custard creams that you eat. I did warn you."

"I don't have toothache; there's nothing wrong with my teeth. And anyway, I don't eat that many muffins or custard creams."

"Hmm? If you say so. I'll give him a call and book a check-up for you after I've made the tea."

"Don't call my regular dentist. I want you to make me an appointment with a Mr Tist."

"I thought you liked your current dentist?"

"I do. This is in relation to a case I'm working on. When you book the appointment, tell them I've just moved to the area, would you?"

"Okay, dear. I'll get straight on it."

"You're very welcome," Winky said. He looked very pleased with himself.

"What are you talking about? It's too early for cryptic conversations."

"Is that all the thanks I get for clearing up that mess out there?"

"You did that?"

"I had a little help, but yes."

"You got rid of all the dead plants?"

"And the dead locusts, and all the other mess that was left behind. You'd never know the jungle had been there."

"I don't know what to say."

"How about: Thank you, Winky?"

"Err—thank you, Winky." I walked over to my desk, and then it struck me. "Hold on. I suppose you're going to bill me for all of this, aren't you? How much is it going to cost me?"

"That is so very hurtful." He clutched his heart. "Why would you say something like that? I was happy to do it for my good friend."

"So, there's no charge?"

"None."

"In that case, I'm sorry for what I said. That's very kind of you. Thank you."

Maybe I'd misjudged him? Maybe underneath that brash exterior, he really was a kind-hearted soul.

What are you lot laughing at?

***

According to the wicked witch-wannabe who worked in Shiny Shiny, the lowlife who was peddling the starlight fairy wings was scheduled to pay the shop a visit at eleven o'clock. I'd taken cover in the doorway of a vacant shop that was more or less straight across the road from Shiny Shiny.

When he arrived, the salesman was wearing an ill-fitting suit. The trousers were an inch too short; the sleeves were an inch too long. I wasn't sure if he was going for the 'hipster' look, or if he'd bought the mismatched jacket and trousers from a fire sale. My money was on the latter. For reasons known only to him, he had the back of his collar turned up. But it was his battered briefcase that really gave him away.

To make absolutely sure I had my man, I made my way across to Shiny Shiny, and peeped through the window. The man had his suitcase open, and was pointing to the display of fairy wings on the counter. That confirmed it— this was my man.

Twenty minutes later, when he re-emerged, I followed him back to the multi-storey car park. His car was as classy as his suit. For some reason, he'd felt the need to add wide wheels, and a dual exhaust system. Nothing wrong with that you might think, but he was driving a Reliant Robin. Seriously?

"Excuse me, sir?"

He almost dropped the briefcase.

"You scared me to death, lady."

"Sorry. Look, I'll be honest. I've just followed you in here."

"Really?" His face lit up, and his smile revealed a number of gold teeth. "And what's your name, gorgeous?"

"I wouldn't want you to get the wrong idea. My interest in you is purely on a business basis."

"Oh?"

"I'll be opening a small shop soon: Jewellery, trinkets, that kind of thing. I've seen the fairy wings that Shiny Shiny stock. They're beautiful, and I believe you supply them?"

"What's the name of this shop of yours?"

"Like I said, it isn't open yet, but it'll be called — err — Pretty, Pretty, Pretty."

"That's a lot of pretties."

"Do you like it?"

"It's okay." He shrugged.

"I'd like to make sure I have the fairy wings in stock when I open. I'm willing to place a big order. Can you help?"

"Sure. Why not?" He placed the briefcase onto the roof of the car, and flicked open the catches. "Beautiful, aren't they?"

"They really are, but they were a lot more beautiful when they were attached to the fairies you killed to get them."

He slammed the case closed. "Who are you?"

"Your worst nightmare."

I used the 'tie up' spell to bind him hand and foot, then I pushed him and his case into the back seat of the car.

"Daze, it's Jill. There's someone here I think you'd like to meet."

Chapter 22

"I've booked you an appointment with the new dentist, Jill. It's this afternoon. I hope that's okay?"

"That's fine. Thanks, Mrs V. The plants look nice."

"They do, don't they? They cheer the place up no end. Would you like a drink?"

"No, thanks. I'm not going to be here for long. I'm meeting the colonel, shortly."

"The colonel?" She looked confused. "But isn't he—err—I thought he was dead?"

Oh bum!

"Sorry. Slip of the tongue. I meant to say that I'm going to the colonel's old house. I have a meeting with the new owner."

"That pop star man? The one with the silly name?"

"Murray Murray? Yes, that's the guy."

"I imagine seeing the old house again will bring back memories of the colonel. You must still miss him?"

"Yes, but then in a funny way, it feels like he's still around."

"It's curious you should say that because ever since we visited the old sock factory, I've felt a—err—" She glanced around. "I suppose you'd call it a presence."

"Like a ghost, you mean?"

"Yes. I wonder if it's that long-lost ancestor of mine, trying to get in touch?"

"Socky?"

"What did you call him?"

"I—err—I meant Tobias. From ye oldie *sockie* factory."

Winky was fast asleep under the sofa. Bless his little

cotton socks. He was such a kind, considerate cat, and obviously loved me dearly.

Mrs V appeared in the doorway. "Jill, there's a man out here. He says he has something for a Mr W. Inky. I told him there's no one of that name here. Do you want me to tell him to go away?"

"No, it's okay. Send him through."

"Package for Mr Inky." The young man had his index finger stuck up one of his nostrils.

So classy.

"I'll give it to him."

"I don't know about that. I was told to hand it to Mr Inky."

"Mr Inky is my—err—partner. You can leave it with me."

"Okay, then." He thrust it into my hand, and then left—finger still firmly up his nostril.

It's not that I was nosy. Because you know me—I have never been, and will never be nosy. I am, however, very security conscious. The small package wrapped in brown paper looked rather suspicious to me, so it behoved me (Behove? Good word, eh?) to ensure it didn't represent a threat to my darling cat.

For that reason and that reason only, I took a quick look inside.

What the—?

It was full of ten-pound notes. Three hundred pounds in total. With them was a scribbled note: *£300 for the plant pots, as agreed. Phil the Plant.*

"Winky!"

"Where? Who? What?" He came stumbling out from

under the sofa.

"Who is Phil the Plant?"

"Oh."

"You might well say 'oh'. I thought you had cleaned up the outer office out of the goodness of your heart?"

"I did."

"Not to sell the plant pots, then?"

"Throwing them away seemed a waste."

"They should have been returned to Rodney."

"The old bag lady's bit on the side?"

"Mr Greenfinger is not Mrs V's *bit on the side.*"

"So she says. Anyway, what's done is done. Hand over the cash."

"No chance. I'm going to give this to Rodney."

"Wait! Don't do that. What about the costs you incurred getting rid of the locusts?"

"That's true."

"And the cost you would have incurred if I hadn't handled the clean-up operation?"

"Also true."

"In that case, let's split the cash fifty, fifty?"

"Why shouldn't I just keep it all?"

"Because I may have information from my people regarding a certain Detective Riley."

"Do you?"

"I think so, but my memory is a little hazy."

"Would half of this cash help to clear your mind?"

"I think it might."

I counted out half of the money, and handed it to my cold, calculating cat.

"So? What did your guys find out about Leo Riley?"

"He's met with several people over the last few days,

but there's one in particular who will interest you, I believe."

"Who is it?"

He fished out his phone, and held it up for me to see.

"Martin Macabre!"

I should have known. That scumbag Riley had to be on the take. It was the only thing that made any sense. Why else would he care whether or not I had an animal in here?

"Did I do good or what?" Winky tweaked his whiskers.

"You did. Thanks."

"You could show me your gratitude by handing over the rest of the cash."

"I'm not that grateful."

So, Riley was taking backhanders from my landlord. I'd never liked him, but I hadn't realised just how low he was prepared to stoop. What should I do about it? If I told Jack, he'd want to get involved, and I couldn't have that. Riley was my problem, and I intended to deal with him, but it would have to wait because I was due at the colonel's house.

I was just on my way out when my office door burst open. It was Ma Chivers, and she was blue.

By that, I don't mean she was sad; I mean she was the colour blue — as far as I could tell, from her head to her toes.

"Sorry, Jill." Mrs V appeared behind her. "This *lady* just pushed her way in."

"That's okay, Mrs V. I'm never too busy to see a Smurf."

Mrs V backed out, and left us alone. Winky shot for cover under the sofa.

"This is your doing!" she yelled. "You and your

grandmother."

"I have no idea what you're talking about. Would you like me to turn up the heating? You seem to have turned blue from the cold." With that, I dissolved into laughter.

"Laugh while you can. I'll make sure you and Mirabel pay for this. You see if I don't." And with that, she turned around and stomped out, slamming the door behind her.

Grandma had said that I'd know when the 'bounceback' spell had kicked in. She hadn't been kidding.

***

The colonel's old house was looking as good as ever. There were no other cars parked on the forecourt; hopefully, that meant the colonel had been right about Murray Murray being out for the afternoon.

As I approached the door, it swung open.

"Hello?" I called from the doorstep.

"Come in, Jill. We're over here."

I stepped inside and found the colonel and Priscilla standing at the bottom of the staircase.

"Hi, Priscilla. Long time, no see."

"Hello, Jill. Come with me. We'd better hurry."

"Sorry? What are we doing?"

"You're supposed to be the Lady of the Manor. You can't greet your visitors dressed like that."

"What's wrong with these clothes?"

"You look like the hired help," the colonel said. "Hurry up. Cilla knows what she's doing."

It was pointless arguing, so I followed Priscilla upstairs, into one of the bedrooms.

"There you are." She pointed to the elegant dress that

was lying on the bed. "I think I've got the size right, but you'd better try it on."

I did, and it was a perfect fit. I'd never worn anything quite so posh.

"You look great," Priscilla said. "The shoes are over there."

As we made our way back downstairs, the colonel nodded his approval. "Simply top notch! Now, what will you call yourself?"

"Jill?"

"No, that won't do at all. Let me think. I know—you should introduce yourself as Lady Raybourn. And don't slouch. A *lady* never slouches."

"Don't slouch? Okay, got it."

And not a moment too soon because just then there was a loud knock at the door.

"It's a pity we couldn't have organised a butler for you," the colonel said.

"I'll be fine. Wish me luck."

The colonel and Priscilla made themselves scarce. I took a deep breath, and opened the door.

"Hi, we're from Hauntings Unlimited. You're expecting us, I believe?"

"Indeed I am." I was doing my best to speak with the proverbial plum in my mouth. "Do come in."

The two vampires were younger than I'd expected: one very tall, the other no taller than me.

"I'm Alexander, and this is Maurice. I hadn't realised you were a sup."

"Is that a problem?"

"Not at all. We have several clients who are sups. I'm very sorry, but the message you left didn't mention your name?"

"Lady Raybourn."

"Pleased to make your acquaintance, your ladyship." Alex bowed.

"How did you come to hear of our service?" Maurice asked.

"A friend. I don't recall who, now. I attend so many functions and parties, they all blur into one another."

"Of course. And what exactly is it you're looking for?"

"This magnificent house costs a small fortune to maintain, and we rely entirely on the revenue generated by visitors. The problem is that the numbers have dropped off over recent years. I'm looking for ways to rekindle the interest, and get more visitors through the door."

"You've come to the right place. Nothing is guaranteed to stimulate interest more than the news that the house is haunted."

"I'm still a little sceptical. Don't ghosts scare people away?"

"You might think that, but it isn't the case. Our own records show that visitor numbers increase by as much as three hundred per cent once word gets out that a house is haunted."

"Really? That is very impressive. How exactly does it work?"

"We specialise in long term hauntings, and specifically to the customer who wants to have the house haunted all year around."

"That's certainly the kind of thing I'm looking for."

"Great. How many rooms do you want to be haunted? Some customers require haunting of just a single room, others require several rooms to be covered."

"Hmm? I hadn't really thought about that. Probably two or three of the larger rooms."

"The other thing we need to know is the kind of ghosts you'd require. If you have no particular preference, the cost will be lower. The more specific you wish to be, the higher the cost."

"Could you give me a ballpark figure? Let's say three large rooms with a mix of ghosts—haunted all year around?"

"Off the top of my head, you'd be looking at six ghosts—two per room. Total cost would be ten-thousand pounds a month."

"That's an awful lot of money."

"Not really. Not when you consider that the majority of that goes to the ghosts themselves. It's only because you're a sup that we can tell you that. If you were one of our human customers, we'd have to say that the costs were to cover the special effects which create the ghost illusion."

"Let me make sure I understand this correctly. You're saying that over half of the fee paid to you is passed on to the ghosts themselves?"

"That's correct."

"In that case, how come so many ghosts in GT are up in arms over non-payment of wages?" I'd abandoned the posh voice. "Isn't it true that you're actually pocketing most of the money for yourselves?"

They both looked as though they had had the wind knocked out of them. Alex was the first to recover.

"Who are you, really?"

"My name is actually Jill Gooder."

"I've heard of you. You're the one who can travel to GT."

"That's right. I've been retained by a large number of your disgruntled employees to find out why they aren't being paid."

"But we are paying them. Every month on the dot, we send the money through to our partner in GT."

"Kelvin Toastmaster? I've met him. He insists the money never reaches him."

The two vampires were stunned into silence for several moments.

"He's lying," Maurice said, at last. "And we can prove it. If you come to our offices, we can show you our bank accounts; they detail every payment made."

"Are you saying Toastmaster is pocketing the money?"

"He must be. We had no idea there was a problem with the payments. We knew we were losing far more staff than we should be doing, but Kelvin told us it was because they didn't like the work. Just wait until I get my hands on him."

"Hurting him won't get the ghosts the money they're owed. Leave it with me. It's time I had another chat with our Mr Toastmaster."

"Don't you want to see our bank accounts?"

"No need. The fact you offered is good enough for me. For now, at least."

I made a call to Winky.

And yes, I do know how weird that sounds.

"It's Jill?"

"Whatsup?"

"I need you to get that hacker friend of yours to check

something for me. What's his name? Tabby?"

"Tibby the Hack."

"That's the guy. Listen carefully because I need a quick answer on this one."

Chapter 23

Have I ever mentioned that I hate dentists? They're like clowns—evil—all of them. I'd had a check-up at my regular dentist only a couple of weeks earlier, and had been given a clean bill of health, so I knew I didn't need any work doing. Mrs V had managed to get me an appointment with Dennis Tist, under the pretence of my being new to the area. So far, this man was the only common factor that linked all three of the women locked up in Regent's Hospital. If I drew a blank here, I'd be well and truly back to square one.

The receptionist's name was Grace; she had a smile worthy of the job.

"I'll need you to complete this new patient form, please, Ms Gooder." She handed me a tablet, and asked me to take a seat while I entered my details.

"Have you worked here long, Grace?"

"Just under a year. Ever since the practice opened."

"I guess you must be tired of hearing the same joke about your boss's name?"

"Sorry?"

"Mr Tist. Mr Dennis Tist."

"That's his name."

"Yes, I know. Den Tist the dentist?"

She thought about it for a moment, and then the penny seemed to drop. "Oh yes. Of course. Den Tist, the dentist. That's very good. Are you a stand-up comedian or something?"

"Err—no—I'm a—err—chiropodist."

She pulled a face. "Really? I could never do that job. I mean, looking at people's gammy feet all day. Yuk! You must really like feet?"

"Not particularly, but I guess you could say it allows me to *foot* the bills."

"You're so funny. You really should do stand-up."

At last, an appreciative audience. I was warming to Grace.

I'd been expecting Mr Tist to be some kind of monster, but he turned out to be a quite ordinary, clean-cut man in his early forties. I can normally sense whether someone is a human or a sup, but I couldn't tell with this guy.

"Open wide, please."

I did as he requested, and stared up at the TV screen that was fixed to the ceiling, immediately above the dentist chair. The sound was muted, but it was tuned into a channel showing old movies. It took me a few moments to place the movie being screened, but then it came to me: Marathon Man.

"Oh dear." Mr Tist tutted. "Oh dear, oh dear. Not good. Not good at all."

Now, I'm no expert on matters dental, but I was guessing that wasn't a ringing endorsement. "Is there a problem?" I managed to ask when he removed the mirror from my mouth.

"I'm afraid so, Ms Gooder. One of your canines is in really bad shape. I'm surprised you haven't had any pain."

"I haven't. Not even a twinge."

"That's often the case. One minute everything's fine, the next, wham! Total agony. Don't worry, though, I've had a cancellation, so I can see to it for you now. I'll just knock you out for a few minutes, and when you wake up, everything will be okay."

"Knock me out? Couldn't you just do it with a local anaesthetic?"

"Not for this one. There's going to be a lot of pain. It would be better for you to sleep through it."

"I understood I had to have someone with me if you knock me out? To drive me home?"

"Not with the new anaesthetic we use nowadays. You'll be wide awake and ready to drive within a few minutes." He reached for a needle. "Just a sharp scratch, and then—"

"Sorry." I scrambled out of the chair. "I have an urgent appointment. I can't be late."

"But it will only take a few minutes."

"Sorry. I'll have to come back another time."

"If you don't get it seen to straightaway, you could end up in a lot of pain."

"I'll arrange another appointment with your receptionist. Thanks. Bye."

I hurried out of the surgery, and straight past the reception desk. Once outside, I gave a huge sigh of relief; I felt sure that I'd just escaped something much worse than toothache. There was something very much not right about Mr Dennis Tist. Now more than ever, I believed he could be linked to Jasmine Bold's sudden descent into madness.

***

After that ordeal, I needed something to calm my nerves. What better than a nice cup of tea and a cake? Particularly if it's free.

Who are you calling a cheapskate?

"Are you okay, Jill?" Aunt Lucy was in the kitchen, tidying the cupboards. "You look a little pale."

"I've just had something of an ordeal at the dentist."

"Toothache?"

"No, my teeth are fine. It was to do with a case I'm working on."

"You're okay to eat cake, then?"

"Definitely. You're having a clear out, I assume?"

"Not really. It's my bi-annual cupboard swap."

"What's that?"

"I get fed up with keeping the same things in the same cupboards, don't you?"

"Not really."

"It drives me crazy, so twice a year, I swap everything around."

"Doesn't that make it difficult to find things?"

"It can, but that's all part of the excitement. Lester always complains when I do it, but it's like I told him: best to keep the brain cells active. Now, what kind of cake would you like?"

"What do you have?"

"I'm not sure." She looked up at the cupboards. "Now, where did I put them?"

It took a while, but she eventually found the cakes. I was undecided between the strawberry and the coffee cupcake, so in the end, Aunt Lucy persuaded me I should have both.

What? It was hardly my fault — she'd twisted my arm.

"I hadn't planned on doing the cupboards until next week," Aunt Lucy said. "But with all the rain we've had, it hasn't been fit to do anything in the garden. I heard Grandma had to get you back from CASS recently to sort out the downpour."

"That's right. She has a theory that the torrential rain was actually a ploy to get me back, but I'm not sure I buy it."

"What were you doing there, anyway?"

"Oh, nothing much. Just trying to rearrange the speech I'm going to give to them."

"Did you sort out another date?"

"Not yet. The problem is that it takes so long to go back and forth between here and CASS. Every time I want to go over there, I have to ask the headmistress to arrange tickets for the airship."

"Why don't you try magicking yourself there?"

"I didn't think that was possible."

"It isn't for anyone else, but no one apart from you can magic themselves to GT. Why don't you give it a try? It's not like you have anything to lose."

"Actually, that's not a bad idea. I might just do that."

There was a knock at the door.

"Who can that be?" Aunt Lucy stood up. "I'm not expecting anyone."

Moments later, I heard a man's voice; it seemed somehow familiar.

"Jill, there's a gentleman here to see you. His name is O'Nuts."

"Duncan? How did you know you'd find me here?"

"I asked around to see if you had relatives here in Candlefield. You have such a high profile, it wasn't difficult to trace your aunt. I had intended leaving a message with her, but seeing as you're here, I can thank you in person for everything you've done."

"No thanks necessary. I take it the king of the pixies has been in touch?"

"Arthur? Yes. He's such a gentleman. Not only did he not press charges, he's promised to ensure I have a supply of candles for life — at no cost. I couldn't be happier."

"That's great news. I guess there'll be no need to continue with the collections?"

"I'll probably still do them from time to time because there are other costs to cover, but at least the pressure is now off."

"Would you like a drink, Mr O'Nuts?" Aunt Lucy asked.

"No, thanks. I can't stop. Before I go, though, there is one other thing I wanted to mention. I heard that you'd been instrumental in getting that conman locked up; the one with the performing dog. I always thought he was up to no good."

"That's right. The puppies he was selling were actually dog-shifters. They would rob the houses of their new owners, and then make their way back to Candle Sands. My two cousins, Aunt Lucy's daughters, fell for the scam. They're very upset, as you can imagine."

"That's terrible, but maybe I have a way to cheer them up. My dog, Bonny, recently gave birth to a beautiful litter of puppies. We'll be looking for good homes for them in a few weeks. Do you think your cousins would be interested?"

"I'm sure they would. How much would you want for them?"

"Nothing. They'd be doing me a favour, and besides, I

owe you one. Why don't you check with them, and if they are interested, ask them to get in touch with me."

"I will. Thanks, Duncan."

***

I had let Jack know that I would be late home because I wanted to pay another visit to the dentist. I arrived there ten minutes before the official closing time, made myself invisible, and then took a seat in the waiting room. I was quite surprised to find that Grace had already left. At six o'clock on the dot, Tist came out of the surgery, turned off the lights, and left — locking the door behind him. I gave it a few minutes, just in case he'd forgotten anything, then I reversed the 'invisible' spell.

I had no idea what I was looking for, but my instincts told me that there was something strange going on inside that surgery. I couldn't shake the feeling that if I hadn't made my escape when I did, I too might be in a padded room at Regent's Hospital.

For the next hour, I searched every nook and cranny in that surgery, but I drew a blank. Perhaps there was something in the waiting room? As I made my way out of the surgery, I caught my foot on the lever at the base of the dentist chair. As I did, I heard the sound of a motor behind me. When I turned around, I saw the wall slowly sliding open.

It was dark inside the 'secret' cupboard, except for three glowing spots of colour: red, green and blue. I felt inside, and managed to locate a light switch. The cupboard was long and narrow. Along the back wall there was a single shelf on which were three small glass jars. Each of them contained a smoky substance: one red, one green and the other blue. I reached for one with the intention of removing the stopper, but then something made me pull my hand away. I had no idea what I was dealing with, but thought maybe Daze would know, so I gave her a call. She said she'd come straight over.

"Do you have any idea what these are?" I asked.

She nodded. "I've never actually seen them before, but we were taught about this during rogue retriever training."

"What is it?"

"If I'm right, and I think I am, you're dealing with a soul snatcher."

"Are you telling me that these jars contain — ?"

"Souls? Yes, at least I think so."

"I met the guy who is doing this, but I couldn't tell if he was a human or a sup."

"I'm not surprised. Soul snatchers are neither. They're just pure evil. We were told that they should be destroyed on sight because they're much too dangerous to risk locking up in prison."

"I think I know who these souls belong to. The three women in question have been locked up because they're acting crazy."

"I'm not surprised. It's a terrible fate to befall anyone."

"Can it be reversed? Can the women be saved?"

"I'm not sure, but right now, the important thing is that we stop this *creature* before it does the same thing to someone else."

"Okay. What's the plan?"

Chapter 24

The next morning, we were seated at the breakfast bar; Jack was engrossed in his magazine: TPB Monthly.

"Don't you get fed up of reading about ten-pin bowling?"

"Never. There's a fascinating article in this month's edition on how to maximise your spares."

"Sounds unmissable."

"It is. The seven-ten split is the hardest to deal with."

Some days, it was like sharing the house with an alien.

"I've been thinking." I pulled the magazine away from his face. "We ought to go and visit your parents."

"It isn't long since Mum was down here."

"I know, but it's nice to stay in touch."

"You seem awfully keen to see my mum and dad."

"First you complained that we never saw your parents, and now you complain because I suggest paying them a visit. I can't win."

"Sorry. I'm just surprised, that's all. I'll give Mum a call later, and see what I can arrange."

"Good. The sooner, the better."

If Grandma was correct about the witchfinders being mobilised by their new boss, I would need to identify them as soon as possible. Hopefully, Yvonne would be able to help with that.

I made a call to the dentist, and just as I'd hoped, I got the out-of-hours answering machine, on which I left a message:

"Mr Tist, this is Jill Gooder. You were right; I should have had the work done. I've been in agony all night. I'm going to

pop in first thing this morning. Hopefully, you'll be able to sort out this tooth for me. Thanks. See you soon."

"You didn't mention you had toothache." Jack looked concerned.

"I don't. It's all part of the case I was working on last night."

"A dentist? What's he done?"

"I won't bore you with the details, but let's just say he's a nasty piece of work. The man has no—err—"

"Soul?"

"No. He seems to be doing alright for souls. I was going to say he has no scruples."

"That's my girl. Ridding Washbridge of all the bad guys."

"Talking of bad guys, I've discovered that Leo Riley is on the take."

"What? Are you sure?"

"Pretty much. I got it straight from the cat's mouth."

"Shouldn't that be *horse's* mouth? Do you need me to get involved?"

"No. I'd prefer to deal with this one myself."

***

Grace was once again behind reception at the dental surgery. "Hello again, Ms Gooder." She beamed.

I nodded while holding the side of my face.

"That looks painful, but you're in luck. We got your message, and Mr Tist will be able to see you as his first appointment. He'll be with you in about five minutes."

I mumbled a thank you, and then took a seat. If I ever gave up the P.I. gig, I really should consider a career on the stage.

"Morning, Ms Gooder." Mr Tist popped his head around the door. "I'm sorry to say it, but I did warn you. Would you like to come through?"

I followed him inside, and took a seat in the chair.

"Open wide. Hmm, that looks nasty, but not to worry, we'll soon have you feeling as good as new. I just need to send you to sleep for a few minutes." He turned away to get the needle, and as he did, I jumped out of the chair.

"Ms Gooder! I know you're scared, but you really must get back in the —"

I pressed the lever with my foot, and the wall behind him slid open.

"Who are you?" His whole demeanour had changed.

"Who I am doesn't matter. What matters is that you've snatched your last soul."

He dropped the needle, and bolted for the door. When he opened it, he came face to face with Daze, who pushed him back inside.

"Grace!" he yelled. "Call the police!"

"I just gave your receptionist the week off." Daze came in, and closed the door behind her. "And now, it's time for you to say goodbye to this world."

"No, please! Wait!"

Daze took out what looked like a metal tube, which she pointed at the soul snatcher. The blast of energy that shot from it was even more powerful than the 'lightning bolt' spell.

The dentist was no more.

"What about these?" I pointed to the jars. "Can we restore the lost souls to their rightful owners?"

"I wouldn't know where to begin, but I know a man

who might. We can't leave them here, though. Can you take them with you, and keep them somewhere safe?"

"How am I going to carry all three?"

"You'll work something out."

***

"What are those?" Jules pointed to the three jars.

I'd had to call into a coffee shop, and get one of those cardboard tray holders to carry them.

"These?"

"Yeah. They're very pretty. Can I have a look?"

Before I could stop her, she'd grabbed the one containing the blue smoke.

"Be careful. Don't drop it."

"I've never seen anything like this before. Are they for your house? Where are you going to put them?"

"I haven't decided yet. Could you put it back, please?" I had no idea what would happen if the jar broke, and I was in no hurry to find out.

"Do you have any more news on Jasmine, Jill?"

"Nothing I can share with you just yet, but I'm hopeful there may be some good news soon."

After I'd put the jars onto my desk, Winky came sniffing around them. "Is that something to eat?"

"No. Don't go near them."

"What are they?"

"If you must know, they're the souls of three young women."

"Alright, I only asked. There's no need for the sarcasm." Winky took umbrage, and went to sulk under the sofa.

I put the jars in the bottom drawer of my desk, for safekeeping.

It was the first opportunity I'd had to consider what Aunt Lucy had said about CASS. Could I really magic myself there? The possibility had never occurred to me until she suggested it. There was only one way to find out, and that was to give it a try. It wouldn't be easy because the school was a long way away; no more than a tiny oasis in the middle of a vast, unfriendly rainforest.

I spent some time first formulating, and then tweaking and re-tweaking the spell. Once I was happy with it, I summoned up all of my focus, crossed my fingers, and went for it.

I landed with a thud.

Wherever I was, it certainly wasn't CASS. I was surrounded by giant trees, which were so tall that I couldn't see their tops. The sound of a multitude of insects and animals assaulted my eardrums. The heat was unbearable — it was as if I'd stepped into a sauna.

My best guess was that I'd missed the school, and landed in the forest that surrounded it. If I could just get a glimpse of CASS, I should be able to complete my journey, but that would be easier said than done because I could see no further than the trees in front of me. Although there were no paths, the undergrowth to my left did seem less dense, so I started out in that direction. Some of the smaller insects had already found me, and decided that I would make a tasty snack. Trying to swat them all away was an exercise in futility. As annoying as they were, I was far more worried about the larger creatures that inhabited the forest. Their many calls sent shivers down my spine.

After twenty exhausting minutes, I came to a clearing. Although it was good to escape the claustrophobic undergrowth, I felt much more vulnerable in the open. Across the clearing was a hillside. If I could make it to the top, I might be able to get a glimpse of the school. Under normal circumstances, I would have used a spell to speed myself along, but the effort of magicking myself that far had left me exhausted. I didn't want to waste what few reserves of energy I had left because I would need those to get me to CASS or back home.

When I was three-quarters of the way across the clearing, the ground began to vibrate under my feet. I spun around just in time to see a huge creature emerge from the trees. It was an animal I'd come face to face with before: a destroyer dragon. It sniffed the air, and looked around.

Maybe, if I stayed perfectly still, it wouldn't spot me.

Wrong!

It began to charge straight at me. I turned and ran towards the hill, but my legs were so heavy it was like trying to wade through treacle. Even if I made it, I'd never have the strength to climb the hill. Just when I thought I was doomed, I spotted a cave, but could I make it? The footsteps were much louder now — much closer.

When I was a few feet away, I threw myself inside. The dragon's head was too large to get through the entrance, but that didn't stop it from breathing fire into the cave. Fortunately, the cave was deep enough that I was able to get beyond the reach of the flames. After a few minutes, the dragon gave up trying to toast me, but it was still standing right outside the cave.

I was trapped.

Even though I'd been terrified, exhaustion must have overwhelmed me because I'd fallen into a deep sleep. When I woke up, the entrance to the cave was much brighter; the dragon was no longer standing outside. I crept slowly towards the cave mouth, ready to turn and run should the dragon reappear. I took one cautious step outside, and then I saw it, or to be more precise, I saw *them*. The dragon who had almost had me for lunch was now facing off with another destroyer dragon. They were taking it in turns to lunge at one another; neither of them showing any signs of backing down. I must have been asleep for some time because a little of my strength had returned. This was my chance—possibly my only chance.

I began to scale the hillside, watching the two dragons every step of the way. When I'd climbed only a few feet, the first dragon lunged at the other. They were now locked in a deadly battle, clawing and biting one another. Although I hadn't fully recovered, and my body just wanted to lie down and rest, I somehow managed to pick up the pace. I'm not sure how long it took for me to reach the top, but it felt like a lifetime. When I eventually came to a halt, I realised that the sound of fighting had stopped. The first dragon was alone again; he'd seen off his rival, and he was headed my way.

I could now see over the top of the trees, and much to my relief, there in the distance were the walls of CASS. The ground beneath me began to vibrate again, as the dragon reached the bottom of the hill. I had hoped the gradient might put him off, but I was to be disappointed because he began to charge up the slope.

Did I have enough magical reserves to pull this off? Would I get the co-ordinates right this time? There was no time to worry about any of that because in another few seconds I would become a dragon's lunch. I closed my eyes, focussed and cast the spell.

***

Phew! That had been much too close for comfort.

It took me a few seconds to work out where I'd landed, but then I realised I was in the small room that the caretaker, Reggie, had let me into on my previous visit to CASS. Just as before, I couldn't shake the feeling that there was something very familiar about that room. Distant memories danced around my head, but refused to come fully into focus. Voices—two of them—a man and a woman. Who were they? Was the woman me? No, but I felt that I knew her or had some kind of connection to her. I tried desperately to hear what they were saying, but their words were always just out of my grasp. No matter how hard I tried, the memories refused to crystallise, but I couldn't give up on them because I was convinced that there lay the answers I'd been seeking.

That's when I remembered someone I'd met some time ago—in Cuppy C. The lodger who had rented the room above the shop. The snake oil salesman. What was his name? It was something unusual—just a single word. Talbot, that was it. He'd tried to convince me that snake oil was actually a thing, and not the scam I'd always believed it to be. He'd mentioned one type of snake oil in particular; one that was guaranteed to improve your memory. He'd even told me the name of the snake that produced that oil, but I couldn't remember what it was.

If I was ever going to remember what the significance of that room was, who the voices belonged to, and what they were saying, I'd need to track down Talbot, the snake oil salesman.

Chapter 25

I went straight over to Cuppy C; the twins looked much happier than the last time I'd seen them.

"Have you heard, Jill?" Amber gushed. "We're getting puppies!"

"Yes. I was at Aunt Lucy's when Duncan O'Nuts came over."

"We have to wait a few weeks." Pearl had now joined Amber behind the counter. "But it will be worth it. They're adorable."

"That's not our only good news," Amber said. "They've recovered our jewellery. Those slimeballs hadn't had the chance to fence it."

"That's brilliant. I'm really pleased for you both. Do I get a free muffin to celebrate?"

"No, but you can have twenty percent off," Pearl said.

"But that's my usual discount."

"Is it? Oh yes, so it is. Do you still want one?"

"Go on, then. Hey, girls, do you remember the snake oil salesman who stayed here?"

"Talbot? He was okay despite what you might think." Amber passed me the muffin. "Why?"

"I need to get hold of him."

"What for?"

"Nothing in particular."

"Come on," Pearl pressed. "Why do you want to see him?"

"If you must know, I need some snake oil."

The twins laughed, hysterically.

"After everything you said?" Pearl shook her head. "I thought snake oil was just nonsense."

"It probably is, but I still need to buy some."

"What do you need it for?" Amber asked.

"According to Talbot, there's one particular type of snake oil that improves the memory."

"Oh dear." Pearl grinned. "Is old age catching up with you already?"

"Very funny. I can't tell you the reason I need it—not yet, anyway, but it is extremely important. Do you have his details?"

"I don't think he left a forwarding address," Pearl said. "It's possible he left one of his business cards somewhere. I'm not sure."

"Would you mind looking for it when you get a minute? It's really important."

"Okay. If we find it, we'll give you a call."

"Thanks, girls."

"Meanwhile, Jill, would you like to enter our competition?" Amber pointed to a large jar at the far end of the counter.

"What is it?" I moved closer to get a better look. "How many sprinkles are in the jar? I'm good at this type of competition. What's the prize? It's not a giant triangle, is it?"

"Huh? No. The winner gets free muffins for a month."

"That sounds good."

"A maximum of one per day, though."

"Still, that's not to be sneezed at." I studied the jar more closely. "There must be millions in here. It's a good job you took a note of how many were in the packets before you emptied them into the jar."

The twins looked at one another, and their faces fell.

"You did take a note of the number, didn't you?"

They shook their heads.

"Oh dear."

Snigger.

I was still chuckling to myself when my phone rang. It was Daze.

"Jill. I've found someone who might be able to restore the stolen souls. Do you have them somewhere safe?"

"Yeah. They're in my office."

"Good. Can you bring them with you, and meet me and Professor Peesnap later outside Regent's Hospital?"

"Professor Pee—?"

"Snap, yes. He's a wizard who specialises in souls. If anyone can restore them, he can. Shall we say two o'clock?"

"Okay. I'll be there."

***

"Can I help you?" The stern-faced woman behind the reception desk snapped.

"My name is Leo Riley," I said. "I'd like to see Mr Macabre."

In case you were wondering, no, I hadn't lost my mind. I'd used the 'doppelganger' spell to give myself the appearance of my arch-enemy.

"Is Mr Macabre expecting you?"

"No, but please tell him I'm here."

She tutted, gave me the evil eye, but then made the call.

"Mr Macabre will see you." She sounded disappointed; no doubt she'd been looking forward to having security throw me out. "Down there; second door on the right."

I knocked on the door, and entered.

"Leo!" Macabre got out of his chair and came around the desk to greet me. He had a firm if somewhat greasy handshake. "I trust you have good news for me?"

"I assume you're talking about finding evidence that Gooder has an animal in her office?"

"What else am I paying you for?"

"I've had no luck so far, I'm afraid. I'm beginning to think that she doesn't have any animals in there after all."

"So what if she doesn't? You can make it look as though she does, can't you?"

"Are you asking me to fabricate evidence?"

"I'm not asking you to; I'm paying you to. And you won't get the rest of the money until I have the evidence I need to get her evicted. I don't care how you do it."

"Okay. I'll give it another try."

"I don't want you to try, Leo. I want you to succeed. I expect results for my money. Don't come back until you've done it."

"Okay. Bye."

That couldn't have gone any better.

***

Next stop, GT where the woman behind the reception desk at Kelvin Toastmaster's offices was once again going for the bubble gum/fruit combo. This time, though, instead of an apple, she was combining the gum with a pear. It seemed she hadn't quite mastered this new combination because the pear was covered in gum, which she was in the process of peeling off.

I didn't bother asking if I could see her boss because I

didn't want to give him the opportunity to sneak out the back way.

"Hey! You can't go in there!" she yelled, as I breezed past her desk.

"Just watch me."

I burst into Toastmaster's office, to find him watching something on his laptop. Judging by the speed at which he shut it down, I was guessing it wasn't family viewing.

"You can't just come strolling in here."

"I just did. Sorry if I interrupted your — err — *viewing*."

"It was just a wildlife documentary."

"Of course it was."

"What do you want?"

"Lots of things. First of all, I want you to stop being a cheating toerag."

"You can't speak to me like that."

"Next, I want you to give all the money that you've stolen to the rightful recipients."

"I have no idea what you're talking about."

"Don't waste your breath lying to me. You've already done too much of that. I've spoken to your partners, and I've seen their bank records."

"You're taking their word over mine?"

"Correct, and do you know why? I'll tell you. In my game, you build up a lot of contacts. One of my contacts is a master hacker who goes by the name of Tibby. You may have heard of him. Anyway, he was able to hack into your bank account — all of your bank accounts, in fact." I threw a pile of papers onto his desk.

"What are those?"

"Printouts of your recent transactions. Care to take a look?"

He snatched them up, and quickly flicked through them. As he did, the colour slowly drained from his face.

"I never intended for this to happen."

"Of course you didn't. I suppose the money just accidentally jumped into your private accounts. Whoops! There goes another thousand."

"I was short of cash, so I borrowed a little. I intended to give it back, but then —"

"But then you realised you could do it again and again, and you thought you could get away with it. Why worry if a few ghosts don't get paid? There's plenty more where they came from."

"Are you going to hand me over to the police?"

"I should, but that won't get my clients' money back. I'll tell you what's going to happen. First, you're going to pay every one of my clients the money you owe them, and you're going to do it by close of business today."

"I don't have that kind of money."

"According to those print-outs, you do. And secondly, you're going to resign your position with Hauntings Unlimited with immediate effect."

"But I — err —"

"No buts — just do it! I'll check later, and if you haven't done both of those things, you can expect a visit from the police." I started for the door. "And don't even think about doing a runner because I have people watching your offices. Have a nice day."

As soon as I was out of Toastmaster's office building, I made a call to Karen Coombes.

"It's Jill. I have some good news for you."

"I could certainly use some."

"All of the back pay owed to you and your friends should be paid by the end of the day."

"Really? Are you sure?"

"I'm ninety-nine percent certain."

"That's great news. How on earth did you manage it?"

"Kelvin Toastmaster was the one who has been siphoning off the money. I've just persuaded him that it would be in his best interests to hand it over. If you haven't got it by close of business today, let me know."

"That's fantastic, Jill. Thank you so much."

"Also, Toastmaster will be resigning his position at Hauntings Unlimited with immediate effect."

"I suppose that had to happen."

"I thought you'd be pleased?"

"I am, but it's just occurred to me that with Toastmaster gone, the business is effectively no more. A lot of ghosts will be out of work. Still, there's nothing we can do about that. Thanks again, Jill."

Although Karen had been pleased to hear about the back pay, she'd obviously been disappointed about the possible demise of Hauntings Unlimited. But I had an idea—maybe there was a way to keep the company going.

I made a phone call to the colonel.

***

I was due to meet Daze in thirty minutes, but first I had to collect the souls from my office.

"Any update on Jasmine?" Jules asked.

"I'm hoping there'll be some good news by morning. Sorry, I can't hang around. I have to get something from my office, and rush straight back out again."

"No!" I screamed.

Balanced on the edge of my desk were the three glass jars. Standing just in front of me was Winky. He was holding the toy gun I'd left in my desk drawer. My scream must have made him jump because the rubber-sucker dart flew to one side of the desk, and stuck on the window.

"Look what you made me do," Winky complained, as he loaded another dart.

"Give me that!" I snatched the gun from his paws.

"Hey! What's up? I was only having a little target practice."

"Not with those jars, you don't."

"Why not? They're ugly, and you obviously don't like them, or you wouldn't have shoved them in the drawer."

"They're not just jars. They contain souls."

"Why are you still spouting that nonsense?"

"It's true. That coloured smoke is someone's soul."

"Of course it is. And my whiskers are actually made of twenty-four carat gold."

"I don't have time to argue with you." I grabbed the jars.

"At least leave me the gun."

"Don't break anything." I tossed it to him, and then rushed out of the office.

Daze was waiting for me around the back of Regent's Hospital. Standing next to her was a tall, pencil-thin wizard with a white moustache and a brown beard.

"Jill, this is Professor Peesnap."

"Nice to meet you, Professor. Sorry, my arms are rather full."

"Call me PS, everyone does. Let me take one of those."

He took the jar containing the blue smoke; Daze took the one containing the red.

"What's the plan?" I asked.

"Follow me." Daze led the way through the back entrance. Once inside, she took us to a small room on the first floor which was obviously the laundry. "Find a white coat that fits you. No one ever questions someone wearing a white coat."

We did as she said, and then the three of us made our way to the wing where the three young women were being held. No one stopped us, or even questioned us until we reached the entrance to the secure wing.

"You can't go in there," the nurse said.

"This is Doctor Peesnap." Daze stepped forward. "You should have been told to expect him."

The nurse checked her clipboard. "I don't have anything here."

"Check again."

"Still nothing."

"I don't have time for this," PS snapped. "I have a plane to catch in three hours."

"The doctor has flown in specially to see these patients," Daze said. "Do you want to be the one responsible for sending him away?"

"I'm sorry, but without proper authorisation, my hands are tied."

I'd had enough; she wasn't going to budge, so I resorted to the 'sleep' spell.

"Grab her ID card!" I yelled to Daze.

She did, and she used it to swipe us through the door.

"Over here." I'd located the room where Jasmine was

being held. "How do we know which one of these is her soul?"

PS looked at Jasmine through the small window. "Hers is the blue one."

"How can you tell?"

"There isn't time to go into that now."

Daze used the ID card again to gain access to the padded room. She stayed outside while PS and I went in. Jasmine stared at us through the sunken eyes of a mad woman. PS placed the jar containing the blue smoke onto the floor, removed the stopper, and then cast a spell — one I didn't recognise. The smoke spiralled out of the jar and floated towards Jasmine. She opened her mouth as if to scream, and as she did, the smoke disappeared down her throat. I was completely transfixed by what I'd just seen, and somewhat taken aback when a gentle voice said, "Where am I?"

Within minutes, Jasmine was transformed. Her colour had returned, and the light was back in her eyes. Unsurprisingly, she was more than a little confused, so I explained to her that she'd been struck down by a little-known virus. Meanwhile, PS and Daze were returning the souls of the other two women.

At our request, the three women remained in the secure wing, but outside of their padded cells. As far as the young women were aware, we were doctors, so they did as we asked. On our way out, I reversed the 'sleep' spell on the nurse. She would be in for something of a surprise when she went to check on her patients.

"Thanks for your help, PS," I said, once we were back outside.

"Glad to have been of assistance."

"What shall I do with these empty jars?" I asked.

"If you don't mind," PS said. "I'll take them back with me."

"No problem. Do you want to use them for your experiments with souls?"

"Actually, no. I'm planning on making some jam this weekend, and they would be ideal."

After PS had left, I collared Daze. "I see you're still wearing the catsuit. What happened to the plans for the mini-skirts?"

"They've been cancelled."

"How come?"

"All the rogue retrievers threatened to walk out on strike."

"You mean the women?"

"No. Everyone. The women were all set to walk out when the men said they'd come out too in support of us. I have to be honest, I wasn't expecting that."

"Good for them. I for one am glad you're sticking with the catsuit. I've always thought it looked great."

Chapter 26

"I've been thinking," Jack said, in between spoonfuls of muesli.

"About the seven-ten split?"

"No, about you, actually. You really missed your vocation."

"How so?"

"You should have joined the police."

"What makes you say that?"

"You must get fed up with the tedious cases you have to deal with."

"Tedious?"

"Missing people, unfaithful partners, employees embezzling from their employers. It must all be rather boring. You'd have much more interesting stuff to deal with if you'd join the force."

"You're right." I sighed. "I do have to deal with some pretty mundane stuff." Like restoring souls to their rightful owners, returning stolen money from a crooked ghost, helping the pixie king, and breaking up a dog-shifter scam. Just so boring.

"By the way, I spoke to Mum. We can go up there the weekend after next."

"Great. I can't wait to see them again."

The sooner I discovered the identities of the new witchfinders, the better.

***

Miley Riley answered the door.

"Jill? Is Leo expecting you?"

"I doubt it. Can you ask him if he can spare me a few minutes?"

"Sure. Would you mind waiting there?"

"Okay."

Moments later, Leo came outside, shutting the door behind him. He was wearing trousers, and a string vest. Judging by his face, I must have caught him in the middle of shaving.

"What do you want, Gooder? What do you think you're doing coming to my house?"

"I thought you'd prefer me to deal with this away from your workplace."

"Deal with what?"

"Specifically, the fact that you're a corrupt, no-good slimeball."

"You want to watch your mouth or — "

"Or what? Are you threatening me?"

"You bet I am. Just because you're with Maxwell, don't think you can mess with me."

"I've got something I'd like you to listen to."

"What are you talking about?"

I took out the digital recorder, and pressed play.

Riley's face fell as he heard the two voices. "That's not me on there."

"Really? It sounds an awful lot like you. And the other voice is certainly Martin Macabre. How much did he give you, Leo?"

Riley snatched the recorder from my hand, threw it on the floor, and stamped on it.

"I hope you feel better for that. The thing is, I have a dozen copies of that recording."

"What are you planning to do with them?"

"That depends on you. If you put in an immediate transfer request, and you are out of the region within the month, then I might just forget I have the recordings. Otherwise, well, who knows whose desk they may end up on?"

His face was contorted with rage; he clearly wanted to do me some serious damage, but whatever else he was, Riley was no fool. His self-preservation instinct had already kicked in. "Okay. I'll put in a request today, but I can't guarantee I'll be gone within a month."

"I suggest you try. Very hard. For your sake."

***

My phone rang.

"Jill, it's Amber. We've found one of Talbot's business cards."

"That's great."

"His business is called S.O. Enterprises. I've got an address for it here in Candlefield, if you want it?"

"Yes, please. And a phone number if there is one."

As soon as I'd finished on the call with Amber, I tried Talbot's number, but there was no reply, and no answer machine on which to leave a message. The company was located near to Everything Rodent, so I figured I had nothing to lose by going over there on the off-chance that I'd catch Talbot in.

S.O. Enterprises occupied a small office on the third floor. I didn't bother to knock; I just tried the door.

It was open.

Once inside, I could hear noises coming from the other room.

"Hello! Anyone there? Hello?"

"I'm coming." It was Talbot's voice. When he saw me, he grinned. "I wondered how long it would be before I saw you again."

"I did phone, but no one answered."

"I didn't hear it ring, but then I've been in the stock room most of the morning." He brushed the dust off his sleeves. "What can I do for you?"

"You mentioned something about a snake oil to boost memory."

"Surely snake oil is just a big scam? Didn't you tell me so yourself?"

"I still think it is."

"Then why are you here?"

"I'm prepared to be proved wrong. Do you have any of that stuff?"

"You're talking about the oil from the redsnap snake, and yes, you're in luck. I recently received a new batch."

"I'd like to purchase some."

"It's very potent. Can I ask what you intend to use it for?"

"No. That's none of your business."

"Fair enough, but I must warn you that not all memories are good ones. I won't be held responsible for any trauma you might experience."

"I'm prepared to take that risk."

"Okay. Wait here, please."

He disappeared into the back, and returned a few minutes later with the tiniest bottle I'd ever seen. "That will be twenty-five pounds, please."

"How much? That's extortionate."

"Take it or leave it." He shrugged.

What choice did I have? It's not like there were any other snake oil salesmen in the Candlefield Pages.

"Here." I handed over the cash in exchange for the bottle. "How much do I drink?"

"You don't drink it! That could prove lethal. Put a few drops on a handkerchief, and inhale it."

"How long does it take to work?"

"It's pretty much instantaneous, but I have to warn you that the effects will only last for a short time; no more than a few minutes. And under no circumstances must you repeat the dose within a twenty-four-hour period."

"Are there any side-effects?"

"Not usually."

Very reassuring.

***

Had I totally lost my mind? Apparently so because I was seriously thinking about using the snake oil. In fact, I'd been contemplating it for the last twenty minutes—ever since I'd magicked myself over to the small room at CASS.

As soon as I landed there, the feeling that there was something familiar about that room returned, but just as on the two previous occasions, the memories were just out of my grasp. That left me with a stark choice: forget about the stupid room, or inhale the snake oil.

I'd deliberated long enough.

I grabbed a tissue from my bag, sprinkled a few drops of the oil onto it, placed it under my nose, and took a deep breath.

I immediately felt light-headed. My vision became

clouded, but just as quickly, cleared again. I was still in the same room, but now it was furnished. Seated in front of me were two people: a young man with red hair and a red beard, and a young woman. They were the people whose pictures were in my locket. Both of them appeared oblivious to my presence. But of course they were; this wasn't actually happening now — it was just a memory.

"We don't have long," the young woman said.

"I know." The young man took her hand. "My father is still working on the spell. He said it would take another hour."

"We may not have an hour."

Just then, an older woman came through the door. "You both have to leave right now!"

"There's no point, Helen," the young woman said. "My father must know that we're dead. He must see our bodies."

"Is the spell ready?"

"Not yet, but it should be soon."

"What if it doesn't work?"

"Then there's nothing we can do. You must get out of here, Helen. You're the only person other than Damon's father who knows the truth. It's too dangerous for you to stay here."

"I can't leave you, Juliet. Let me stay, please."

"No." The young woman took the locket from her neck, and handed it to the older woman. "Take this. That way we'll always be with you."

They were both close to tears.

The older woman slipped the locket into her bag, and then threw her arms around the young woman. "Take care, Juliet. I love you."

"I love you too, Helen Drewmore. You've been like a mother to me. Now go!"

The figures in front of me seemed to melt away, and the room was once again bare. The snake oil had obviously worn off.

"Jill? How did you get here?" Desdemona Nightowl looked more surprised than angry.

"I magicked myself here."

"Really? No one has ever been able to do that before. But why?"

"There's something about this room that drew me back."

She looked around. "But there's nothing in here."

"Do you know someone called Helen Drewmore?"

"No, sorry. Why?"

"It doesn't matter. Look, I'm sorry to have dropped in unannounced."

"That's okay. Will you join me for lunch?"

"I'm sorry. I can't stay."

I magicked myself back to Washbridge.

My mind was still swirling with what I'd just witnessed. The locket I'd seen given to the older woman was the same one that I had around my neck. And the pictures in that locket were of the young man and woman in the room. I had so many questions: What was the spell that they were waiting for? She'd said her father had to see their bodies—were they planning to commit suicide? And how did I fit into any of this? One person who might have the answers was the old woman, Helen Drewmore, but she must surely be long dead. Maybe she had descendants who would know her story? If I was ever going to solve this mystery, I had to find out what had happened to Helen Drewmore.

***

When I arrived at the office, Jules was beaming.

"You were right, Jill. I had a phone call this morning. Jasmine is much better. They say she can go home from the hospital later today. Carmen and the other woman have made a full recovery too."

"That's great news."

"How did you know she was going to recover, Jill? Did you have something to do with it?"

"Me, no, how could I? I'm not a doctor. I'd just heard on the grapevine that they thought they'd come up with a cure."

It was very chilly inside my office.

"Hello there, Jill." The colonel was sitting on the sofa. Winky was underneath it, shivering from the cold.

"Hi, Colonel. Have you had time to consider what we spoke about on the phone?"

"I have. In fact, Cilla and I spent most of last night discussing it. The business opportunity you mentioned is very different to the one we'd had in mind. We had thought maybe a tea room or coffee shop, but this Hauntings Unlimited business does sound quite intriguing."

"Does that mean you're interested?"

"Possibly, but first we'd like to speak to the people

running the human world end of the business."

"I'm sure that can be arranged."

"Excellent. Assuming those discussions go well, I see no reason why we shouldn't sign on the dotted line."

"Excellent. That's great news for all the ghosts who are already working in haunted houses in the human world. I'd also like you to meet Karen Coombes. She's the one who brought me in on this in the first place. When I spoke to her yesterday, she was rather upset that Hauntings Unlimited might have to close. I'm sure she'll be delighted to hear that you might step in and take over."

"Do you have to bring all these ghosts into the office?" Winky said, after the colonel had left. "This place is like a freezer when they're in here."

"Sorry. How about I buy you a nice cat bed which you can snuggle up in?"

"I like that idea. Make it a double for when Peggy comes over."

ALSO BY ADELE ABBOTT

The Witch P.I. Mysteries
(A Candlefield/Washbridge Series)

Witch Is When... (Books #1 to #12)
Witch Is When It All Began
Witch Is When Life Got Complicated
Witch Is When Everything Went Crazy
Witch Is When Things Fell Apart
Witch Is When The Bubble Burst
Witch Is When The Penny Dropped
Witch Is When The Floodgates Opened
Witch Is When The Hammer Fell
Witch Is When My Heart Broke
Witch Is When I Said Goodbye
Witch Is When Stuff Got Serious
Witch Is When All Was Revealed

Witch Is Why... (Books #13 to #24)
Witch Is Why Time Stood Still
Witch is Why The Laughter Stopped
Witch is Why Another Door Opened
Witch is Why Two Became One
Witch is Why The Moon Disappeared
Witch is Why The Wolf Howled
Witch is Why The Music Stopped
Witch is Why A Pin Dropped
Witch is Why The Owl Returned
Witch is Why The Search Began
Witch is Why Promises Were Broken
Witch is Why It Was Over

Witch Is How... (Books #25 to #36)
Witch is How Things Had Changed
Witch is How Poison Tasted Good
Witch is How The Mirror Lied
Witch is How The Tables Turned
Witch is How The Drought Ended
Witch is How The Dice Fell
Witch is How The Biscuits Disappeared
Witch is How Dreams Became Reality
Witch is How Bells Were Saved
Witch is How To Fool Cats
Witch is How To Lose Big
Witch is How Life Changed Forever

Susan Hall Investigates
(A Candlefield/Washbridge Series)

Whoops! Our New Flatmate Is A Human.
Whoops! All The Money Went Missing.
Whoops! Someone Is On Our Case.

AUTHOR'S WEB SITE
http:www.AdeleAbbott.com

FACEBOOK
http://www.facebook.com/AdeleAbbottAuthor

MAILING LIST
(new release notifications only)

http:/AdeleAbbott.com/adele/new-releases/

Made in the USA
Coppell, TX
05 July 2022